PHILIP BENN

PHILIP BENNION'S DEATH

by

RICHARD MARSH

AUTHOR OF "THE BEETLE: A MYSTERY", "THE JOSS: A REVERSION", "THE DATCHET DIAMONDS", "THE SEEN AND THE UNSEEN", "CURIOS", "THE GODDESS: A DEMON", "A SECOND COMING", &C. &C.

Kansas City:
VALANCOURT BOOKS
2007

Philip Bennion's Death by Richard Marsh

First published as *The Mystery of Philip Bennion's Death*
in 1897 by Ward, Lock and Co. Reprinted as *Philip
Bennion's Death* by Ward, Lock, and Co. in 1899.

First Valancourt Books edition, December 2007
This edition © 2007 by Valancourt Books

Library of Congress Cataloging-in-Publication Data

Marsh, Richard, d. 1915
  Philip Bennion's death / by Richard Marsh. – 1st Valancourt
Books ed.
      p. cm.
  Originally published: London : Ward, Lock, and Co., 1899.
  ISBN 1-934555-30-4
  1. Murder – Investigation. I. Title.
  PR6025.A645P48 2007
  823'.912–dc22

                                                2007042524

Design and typography by James D. Jenkins
Published by Valancourt Books
Kansas City, Missouri
http://www.valancourtbooks.com

CONTENTS

PHILIP BENNION'S DEATH

CHAPTER I

FOUND DEAD

We had been discussing, the night before, De Quincey's essay "On Murder, Considered as One of the Fine Arts." Bennion, in that self-opinionated way which was a characteristic of his, and to which I always objected, maintained that the essayist had not been true to his subject. He had it that the particular case of murder on which De Quincey had founded his paper, was a work of butchery, and not a work of art.

Bennion insisted that murder might be considered as one of the fine arts, possibly as the finest of all the fine arts. But in that case it would have to be regarded from a very different point of view from that in which De Quincey had approached the subject. Bennion observed, and stuck to his observation with all that strength of obstinacy with which he was so divinely gifted, that the artist in murder—the true artist, that is, as distinct from the commonplace butcher—would pay careful attention to particular points. As thus:—

In an artistic murder, Bennion declared, the first thing necessary was to make it appear that there had been no murder at all. There should be no mark of injury upon the corpse, either internal or external; no trace of poison, no suspicion of violence, no sign of a blow. It should seem as if the dead person had been struck down by the visitation of God. The more completely this condition was fulfilled, the more clearly would the artistic sense—in the operator, that is—be evidenced.

Even supposing some person, or persons, suspected that murder had been done, and the exact manner of its doing, still there should be no evidence in existence which should enable him, or them, to prove their suspicions true. And, to go one step farther, should some wholly unforeseen circumstance—the artist in murder would, before all men, know that it is the unforeseen which happens—place in the hands of those suspicious persons something which looked like evidence of guilt, it should still be utterly impossible to father on the criminal his crime.

If, said Bennion, all these conditions were fulfilled, then, and only then, should we see the fine arts applied to murder. His dogmatism half-amused and wholly irritated me, as, indeed, it had a trick of doing. There never was a man like Philip Bennion for laying down what he maintained was the letter of the law. I told him that there was only one person in my acquaintance who had in him the qualities which were required to realise his conception of the artistic homicide.

He indulged in that vulpine distortion of his countenance which he was wont to call a grin.

"You mean my precious nephew?"

I did mean Raymond Clinton, and I told him so. In my opinion there was no crime which would bring him money from which that young man would turn aside.

Bennion rose from his chair. I well remember that he stretched himself, which was another trick he had.

"To tell you the truth, Otway, I am not sure that you are very wrong. I have not myself the highest opinion of my sister's son. Which is the more unfortunate since he is the only relative I have in the world, and—my heir."

He pronounced those last two words, "my heir," with a satiric emphasis which, it struck me, did not augur too well for the prospects of Mr. Clinton.

I never imagined when I parted that night with Philip Bennion, having discussed with him the theory of murder as a fine art, that I should have, in the morning, an instance of murder as a fine art presented to me in actual practice; and, what is more, with the theorist as an example of his theory.

I was at breakfast when Ryan, Bennion's servant, came rushing into my room. He had a face as long as my arm.

"Oh, sir!" he gasped. "The governor!"

I asked him what was the matter with the governor, which was his way of speaking of his master. He never had treated his employer with what I judged to be proper respect, and still Bennion had suffered him.

"He's dead!" gasped Ryan.

"Dead?"

I confess that I was startled; so startled that I rose from my breakfast—which I would not have done for a trifle— and followed Ryan.

Bennion and I shared the same flat in Piccadilly Mansions. Only I had my four little rooms, and Philip Bennion, as became a rich man, had his gorgeous suite. So all I had to do was to follow Ryan across the landing. We entered the room, which was rich with the triumphs of a collector. There, amidst the treasures which would have been welcome in any museum, lay their owner—dead.

Philip Bennion lay on the floor. He lay on his left side. His left cheek was pressed against the carpet, his right cheek was turned upwards towards the ceiling. A pipe lay in front of him, where it had fallen from his nerveless hand. It was one of those gorgeous examples of bygone pipes which he was so fond of collecting and of smoking. It's owner was quite dead. It needed but a momentary examination to show that he had been dead some hours—he was stiff and cold.

"How came you not to discover him before?" I inquired of Ryan.

The man seemed troubled.

"Well, sir, I was out all night, and I've only just come in."

I knew that the man was something of a scamp, and that Bennion had allowed him liberties which I would never have allowed to a servant of mine. Ryan went on:

"It's a fit, sir, isn't it?"

He alluded to the cause of Bennion's death.

"It is murder," I said.

"Murder!" Ryan had been kneeling by the dead man's side. Suddenly he sprang up with a degree of agitation of which I did not think him capable, and which seemed to me unnatural, even under the circumstances of the case. "Murder!" His jaws seemed to be chattering one against the other. "What—what makes you think that?"

I could not tell him what made me think it, though I was as certain it was murder as I was that I myself was still alive. There were no signs of bloodshed. There was nothing which obviously went to prove that he had met his death by sudden violence. He lay as if he had fallen, as Ryan suggested, in a fit. The only peculiarity about his appearance was that his withered, crab-apple countenance was distorted as by a convulsive anguish of sudden pain; as though the death which had come upon him had been unexpected, sudden, fierce, and awful. Beyond that there was nothing in his outward appearance to show that he had not died the natural death which men die in their beds. Yet I knew that Philip

Bennion had met his death in some way by the act of man.

The question which I put to myself as Ryan stood trembling there so that he seemed scarcely able to stand, was, Had I done it? Had I killed this man? It was not an agreeable question to have to put to one's self as one knelt by the dead body of a man whom one had known since one's earliest days. But it was a question to which I had to find an answer, or perhaps some one else might—and an answer which I should not like.

I have, through life, been a victim to that dual state of existence which men call somnambulism. As a somnambulist I am, I suppose, unique. I have been proved to have done things, while fast asleep, which, had they not been proved with strength of proof sufficient to convince even me, I should have deemed incredible. I have written stories and dispatched them to editors while fast asleep, and they have been accepted and paid for. I have saddled horses, and ridden and driven them, while fast asleep. On one occasion, when I was staying in Wales, I got up, dressed myself, and, fast asleep, in the middle of the night ascended Snowdon, only waking to find myself knocking in the early morning at the door of the cottage at the top. A man who would do that, one might say, would be capable of anything, even, in a state of somnambulism, of the murder of Philip Bennion.

Now, after Bennion had left me the night before, I had continued to think of what he had said, in his dogmatic way, of the fine arts as applied to murder. Even after I had retired to rest his words had haunted me in dreams. I had wrestled with nightmare horrors, and I had dreamed that I had gone to Philip Bennion's room and done something to him—even in my dream I knew not what—and said to him: "I will show you the artist in murder." And as I said it he fell back upon the floor. I saw him fall, and I stood and looked upon him as he lay. Then I put out the electric light. I had a clear recollection of putting out the electric light, and then of waking and finding myself in my own bed.

The fact of having put out the electric light—in my dream—was so present to my mind, that now, when wide awake and kneeling by the dead man's body, I noticed that the electric light was out. Who put it out? It seemed sufficiently obvious that Philip Bennion had not. There had surely not been time enough for him to do it, before the end.

It was plain—there was the evidence of the pipe which lay at his side—that in that last dread moment, even, probably, while death was already actually upon him, he had been smoking. I picked up the pipe to make sure. It was full of tobacco. But it had been lighted. Possibly death had overtaken him as he had been indulging in his first whiff. A man does not smoke in his drawing-room—and that museum of curiosities Bennion called his drawing-room—in the dark. The whole building was lighted by electricity. There could be no sort of reasonable doubt that that particular apartment had been illuminated by the electric light when Philip Bennion had lighted his last pipe. And the first whiff of that last pipe had brought him death. Who—after he was dead—had put out the light? I had dreamed that I had done so. Had it been more than a dream? Had I done, in reality, what I imagined I had only dreamed?

I am free to own that I put the question to myself with a sense of considerable discomfort. I had done some queer things, in my time, when fast asleep; but I had never before got so far as murder. I am not, so far as I am aware, a man of homicidal tendencies. But what psychologist shall tell us what changes take place in a man's nature when he passes from wakefulness to sleep?

I put a question to Ryan.

"Did you turn off the light?"

He stared at me askance, with an evident lack of comprehension.

"When? I was out all night. I have only just come in."

"I mean, did you turn it out when you just came in?"

"Turn it out? It was out. It was broad day."

The fellow evidently missed the point. It was plain, if the light was out when Ryan entered, that some one had been in the room since Bennion's death and turned it out. It struck me that a judge and jury would consider that the case looked ugly against that person, whoever he might chance to be. He could not have failed to notice that motionless form lying there, in its awful eloquence, and why had he not given the alarm? Yes, why?

And the worst of it was that I had such a vivid consciousness of having, in my dream, looked down upon Bennion, silent on the floor—my God! just as he was silent now—and of then moving two or three paces from him, touching the electric button, and plunging the whole room into darkness. If this had been more than a dream, what ought I to do? In any case, what ought I to do?

I imagine that Ryan mistook the horror which began to settle on my mind, as I mentally contemplated the extraordinary nature of the situation I was in, for the stupor of grief at the death of my old friend. Because I became conscious that he was regarding me with what seemed to me to be extraordinary intensity. I was about to make some remark, anything, as it were, to break the spell—the spell of horrid silence—when the door opened, and Raymond Clinton entered.

CHAPTER II

MR. CLINTON

I AM willing, at the outset, to own that I always did have an intense objection to Mr. Raymond Clinton. The objection extends to the whole class of men of which he was but a type. Personally, Mr. Clinton was something under thirty years of age, tall, slight, and, I believe, by some women esteemed good-looking. He was what used to be called a "swell," but what, I understand, in the current slang of the day is called a "chappie." I have no notion what that sort of person will be called to-morrow, but I know that he will be, as he always has been, a fool.

Mr. Clinton was left a small fortune on the death of his mother. But that soon went, if it had not gone before he had it. Then his uncle made him a regular allowance, which was as regularly exceeded. Philip Bennion was always giving him a helping hand out of financial ditches. I strongly suspect that he was in a very tight place at that particular moment, and that he had been making overtures, and hitherto unsuccessful overtures, to his uncle for assistance. Raymond Clinton, I was always convinced, had in him, as is the case with most fools, the making of a first-rate rogue; a finer natural liar, on his own lines, I never yet encountered. In dealing with him, the best thing was to take it for granted that he was always lying, and even then he deceived you by lapses into truth.

He stood in the open door leaning on his stick, his glass in his eye, as if he were at a loss to understand my presence, at that hour, in Philip Bennion's room.

"Hallo, what are you doing here?" He spoke in that

lifeless drawl which he so much affected. Then he caught sight of what was lying on the floor. As he did so, a marked change took place in his looks and his bearing. Staggering slightly forward, he clutched at the back of a friendly chair. "Hallo," he repeated, "what are you doing here?"

As I marked, what seemed to me, the evident effort which he made to appear at ease—and, as a rule, no man needed to make less effort in that direction, a cooler, easier-going, more impertinent scamp than Raymond Clinton never lived—an instant conviction entered my mind that either he or I had slain old Bennion. The unfortunate part of the matter was that the conviction went no further than it did. The balance of probability was against Mr. Clinton. But then, what could a man think who knew himself to be a somnambulist, and who had dreamed, in the silent watches of the night, the dream which I had dreamed?

I stood up. I looked Mr. Clinton intently in the face. I pointed to the dead man lying on the floor.

"Mr. Clinton, do you not see who is lying here?"

"Gracious!" He said, "gwacious," but I do not wish unnecessarily to emphasise his continued and, apparently, constitutional misusage of his mother tongue. "It's old Ben! How doosed funny!"

"What is deuced funny, Mr. Clinton? Your uncle is dead."

"Dead!" Mr. Clinton dropped into the chair, the back of which he had been clutching. In spite of his affectation of surprise—which, by the way, was very badly done—something told me that he had been well aware of his uncle's death, not only before my statement of the fact, but before he had entered the room. "How doosed odd!"

I will do him the justice to say that he never made the slightest pretence at sorrow; but, as he sat there, focussing me with his eye-glass, he seemed to become conscious that something else was demanded of him besides a mere empty exclamation. So he gave vent to his feelings in these eloquent words:

"Poor old cock!" He paused; then added: "What's he died of?"

I purposely waited a moment or two before I answered.

"Your uncle, Mr. Clinton, has been murdered."

I had hit him hard. He showed more signs of being moved than, in one of his lymphatic nature, I had thought was possible.

"Murdered!" He stood up; he let his stick fall to the ground. Unless I am much mistaken he changed colour. "Gracious!"

There was silence for a moment or two. I never took my eyes from off his face. Conscious that this was so, he looked in every direction but towards me. I could see that he was trembling. I could also see that he was making a strong attempt to preserve his self-control. At last, removing his hat, for the first time he moved to where the dead man lay. He stood looking down at him.

"Has he been shot, or stabbed, or what?"

"That remains to be seen."

He glanced up at me.

"What do you mean?"

"The exact kind of foul play by which your uncle met his death remains to be shown. And it will be shown, just as surely as they will find his murderer."

"Then you are not certain he was murdered?"

"I am certain. I am as certain your uncle was murdered as I am certain that you are standing there."

He continued to glance at me a moment longer. Then he turned to Ryan.

"What do you think?"

"I think, sir, and so I've told Mr. Otway"—there was a certain doggedness in the fellow's tone—"that the governor's died in a fit."

Mr. Clinton at once chimed in with Ryan's suggestion.

"Of course he's died in a fit. Who'd want to murder him?" He looked up, as it seemed to me, with defiance in his eyes. "You'll see that's what the doctors will say—that he died in a fit."

CHAPTER III

THE VERDICT

Mr. CLINTON proved a true prophet. That was what the doctors did say—that Philip Bennion had died in a fit. And, practically, that was the verdict of the coroner's jury too.

I attended the inquest, though I was not called as a witness. Mr. Clinton also attended the inquest, though he was not called as a witness. I wish he had been. I would have given a good round sum out of my own pocket to have seen and heard him answer a few questions put to him by a good cross-examining counsel. From my point of view, it seemed to me that the whole affair of the inquest was a farce. What was more, when I thought things quietly over by myself, I did not see what grounds I had to go upon which would enable the inquiry to take a wider range. I could scarcely volunteer to go into the box and detail the conversation which Philip Bennion and I had had upon the art of murder the night before he—died. What good purpose would it serve? What were the deductions which I drew? That Philip Bennion followed up a conversation on murder as one of the fine arts by committing suicide? Without proofs, the thing seemed preposterous on the face of it. And yet I, who knew Philip Bennion better than any man in the world, was quite conscious that that was just the sort of thing which he was capable of doing, if only for the sake of puzzling me with a psychological problem. Should I go into the witness-box, and, having mentioned that I was a somnambulist, tell the story of my dream? Not to dwell on the fact that no man is bound to criminate himself, what shred of evidence had I, somnambulist or no somnambulist, that, on that particular occasion, my dream had been anything but a dream?

No. The question which had to be answered was the question as to how Philip Bennion met with his death. That question the doctors alone could answer. And they did answer it, in their own fashion. They declared that he had died, as Ryan phrased it, in a fit. The trouble was the heart. It was not quite clear what the precise nature of the trouble was, but the general consensus of medical evidence seemed to show that Philip Bennion had died of valvular disease of the heart.

Ryan was the first witness who was called. He stated that, on his entry into the drawing-room, he perceived his master lying on the floor. When it transpired that this was a few minutes after eleven o'clock, the coroner asked him, rather sharply, as I had asked him, how it was that he had not discovered his master sooner. It then came out that he had been absent throughout the night, and had only just returned. When asked if this had been with his master's permission, Ryan hesitated, and then owned that his master had known nothing at all about it. The admission created, what the newspapers call, a "slight sensation." Ryan, in dogged tones, went on to state that he had been in Philip Bennion's service nearly thirty years, and that he had been in the habit of spending a night out, now and then, "when he thought he would." This I knew myself to be true, though Ryan might have added that there always ensued a row royal with his master in the morning.

In answer to further questions, Ryan went on to state that he had no reason to suppose that his master had ever meditated suicide; that he was a sharp-tempered "gent," who said what he meant, and more than he meant, at times, but that, so far as he was aware, he had not an enemy in all the world.

"He was as kind and generous a gent, at bottom, in spite of all his sharp ways, as ever lived." Such was the post-script to his evidence which Ryan added of his own accord.

The next witness was Bennion's own medical adviser, Fullalove Carter. He stated, what was news to me, that he had suspected for some time that his patient's heart was weak. He had made an examination, and he was of opinion that Philip Bennion had died of valvular disease of the heart. There might, or might not, have been some exciting cause, such, for instance, as a sudden shock. But it was well known that, in the case of a person with a weak heart, no exciting cause was absolutely needed, and that death was often, as it were, spontaneous. At the same time, he was bound to add that there were certain peculiarities about the case which had induced him, while making his post-mortem examination, to solicit the assistance of the eminent authority on diseases of the heart, Dr. Blakeham Warner.

Dr. Blakeham Warner, the eminent specialist thus referred to, followed Dr. Carter. He was inclined to be ultra-scientific. It seemed to me that he was more than half disposed to favour the court with a little learned medical disquisition on the human heart in general, and on Philip Bennion's heart in particular. The coroner had some difficulty in keeping him to the point. One thing was plain, that Dr. Blakeham Warner regarded Philip Bennion's as a particularly interesting "case."

He had never seen a human heart present, in some respects, so peculiar an appearance as Philip Bennion's. The peculiarity consisted in the appearance it presented of extraordinary and violent constriction. It was difficult to say as to what such an appearance might be owing. There were features about it which, in his experience, were unique. He detailed these features at considerable length—at rather more length, indeed, than the coroner seemed to relish. They might be owing to organic disease, or they might be owing to the action of certain poisons. Here I pricked up my ears, and I saw that Raymond Clinton pricked up his. As, for instance, such a poison as hydrocyanic acid. For himself, the attitude of his mind was an open one. He should like to hear what were the results of the analysis. If the presence of no poisonous matter was proved, and the other organs of the body were in a healthy condition, then he should say that the cause of death was valvular disease of the heart, though it was attended with features and certain peculiarities—on which, if the coroner had not stopped him, he seemed again disposed to enter into detail—which, in his experience, were unique.

The next witness was, in a certain sense, my witness. I had insisted on the contents of Philip Bennion's stomach being sealed up and forwarded, for analysis, to the famous toxicologist, Lewis Cowan. Mr. Cowan, when he appeared, made short work of the matter. The manner in which he gave his evidence was in striking contrast to the manner in which Dr. Blakeham Warner had given his. He came at once to the point. He stated that he had discovered nothing; that there was nothing to discover; that Philip Bennion had not died of poison; that there was not the slightest trace or suspicion of any sort of injurious matter to be found; that the contents of his stomach had been in a perfectly normal and healthy condition.

On that evidence the coroner briefly charged the jury. After a momentary hesitation they returned a verdict of "Death from natural causes." As they did so, Raymond Clinton looked up at me with what was unmistakably a gleam of triumph in his eyes. As I was leaving the room in which the inquiry had been held, he came and whispered in my ear: "I told you so."

And I felt that the first condition of Philip Bennion's artist in murder had been fulfilled; that the criminal had wrought his crime with such ingenuity and skill as to leave upon the body of his victim no trace of the deed which he had done.

CHAPTER IV

NINA PAYS ME A VISIT

THAT same day Nina Macrae came to see me. Bennion and I had been left as her trustees and guardians under her father's will; but as I had felt that, for many reasons, Bennion had been more capable of filling such a trust than I, I had practically left the whole management of the young lady and her fortune in his hands. Thus she had come to look upon him, in many respects, almost in the light of a second father.

I had not thought proper to acquaint her of the untoward fate which had overtaken Philip Bennion; still, I had expected that she would have heard of the affair from other quarters. But now, to my surprise, she declared that she had only chanced upon the news by accident.

She stood, holding the handle of the door in her hand, looking down at me. The young women of England are certainly growing taller every year. I am not a dwarf, yet Nina Macrae is a good half-head taller than I am.

"Mr. Otway, what is the meaning of this?"

I knew very well what she referred to, but I dissembled.

"The meaning of what, my dear?'

"Guardian's dead! Is it true?"

She saw the answer in my face. She came hurriedly forward.

"Oh, Mr. Otway, why did you not tell me?"

I wished then that I had told her; but I did not say so.

"There were reasons, my dear."

"Reasons! What reasons?"

I did not choose to tell her what the reasons were—that I had suspected foul play, and wished to keep the knowledge from her as long as possible; still less did I choose to tell her that my mind had been so engrossed with other matters that I had scarcely thought of her at all.

"There were reasons, my dear, although just now I am not able to speak of them to you."

She stared at me.

"Guardian—dead!" She sank down into a chair, looking as though she were unable to realise the thing. "I was just coming to see him." There was a sort of catching in her breath, but she did not cry. The young women of England are not only growing taller, but it seems to me that they are growing less tearful too; both of which changes, to my mind, are for the better. The young women of my day used to cry for nothing at all, in pailfuls. It requires something, now-a-days, to make their daughters shed a tear. "I have had a letter from Ralph. He has sent a message for guardian. I was coming to bring it." She dropped her voice. "Mr. Otway, what did guardian die of?"

"The doctors say that he died of heart disease."

I suppose there was something in the tone of my voice which struck her ear.

"The doctors say. What do you mean? What do you say?"

I did not choose to tell her what it was I thought.

"I say what the doctors say—that Philip Bennion, my old friend, in the seeming prime of his health and vigour, was suddenly taken away."

She looked at me as though she were trying to read in my face more than my words conveyed.

"I suppose you are my guardian now?"

"I always have been your guardian. Only, hitherto,

I have left the reins of guardianship in wiser hands than mine. I have felt that a young lady and her fortune might prove more than I could manage. Now I must do my best to do the best for, and with, both."

I do not know what moved her, but without any warning, all at once rising from her chair, she crossed the room and kissed me; she had to stoop to do it, too.

"Is it true there was an inquest?"

"Yes, my dear, it is quite true. The inquest was held this morning. The fact that it was necessary to hold an inquest was one of the reasons why I did not acquaint you sooner with the news that my old friend was dead. So far as we know, no human eye was the witness of his death. Under such circumstances, the English law insists that inquiry shall be made into the cause of death."

"And what was the verdict?"

It seemed to me that her voice betrayed acute anxiety.

" 'Death from natural causes' was the verdict of the coroner's jury."

"Natural causes. Oh?" She gave a sigh of evident relief. "Poor guardian! I shall call you guardian now."

I thought of "the king is dead—long live the king," and bowed.

"My dear, I shall feel highly flattered."

"And to think that I should only have had a letter from Ralph this morning, containing one of those funny messages of his for guardian. It seems that he has discovered some wonderful curiosity in the bric-à-brac way—a snuffbox, I think it is—which I was to tell guardian all about, just, as Ralph says, to make his mouth water."

"Where is Ralph?"

"He was in Rome when he wrote me. He had been in Rome nearly a fortnight. Poor Ralph, how grieved he will be!"

I thought it probable that he would be grieved, in a measure. Ralph Hardwicke was as fine a young man as I ever met. With a sufficiency of means, and a sufficiency of brains to enable him to use them to the best advantage. High-spirited, full of life, and fun, and frolic. He presented that, unfortunately, unusual combination—he was a clever young man and a good young man; straight as a die, without a suggestion of priggishness or pharisaical impertinence. He was handsome, tall, and strong, an athlete, and a scholar. What, I believe, commended him to Philip Bennion, as much as anything else, was his taste for bric-à-brac. Bennion had owed some of his rarest treasures to young Hardwicke's keen scent, and to his unerring judgment, when it came to be a question of a genuine piece of *vertu*. Certainly Bennion had regarded Hardwicke, I verily believe, with more affection than the average father regards the average son. He had known him from his earliest childhood, he had been his guardian until he reached man's estate, and I had reason to believe that, through life, Hardwicke had made of him his constant and his closest confidant.

Nina Macrae, too, regarded Mr. Hardwicke with a favourable eye, just as Mr. Hardwicke regarded her. They had both been Philip Bennion's wards, and they had grown up together almost as sister and brother. But they had come to regard each other with a more than sisterly and brotherly love. I was as certain as I was certain of anything that she worshipped the ground on which he stood, just as he returned the compliment by worshipping the ground she trod upon. So far as I knew, there had been no open declaration of affection, and there had certainly been nothing in the shape of an open engagement. And this had rather surprised me, because, although Nina was only nineteen, Ralph was four or five-and-twenty. There could scarcely have been a match more to Philip Bennion's liking, and it would have only needed a word from him—at least, so it had always seemed to me—to have had the matter signed, and sealed, and settled.

CHAPTER V

I VISIT MR. CLINTON

IT was about a week after the inquest, and Nina Macrae's visit to me, that a very curious thing happened—so curious a thing that it impressed me almost as much as I had been impressed by circumstances attending my old friend's death.

I was coming up the stairs which led to Piccadilly Mansions, when I met Raymond Clinton, who was coming down them. He stopped me, and to my, I have no doubt, unequivocal surprise, asked me if I would drop into his rooms after dinner for a chat. He had, he said, something which he wished to say to me. I wondered what he could have to say which could be of interest to me—except upon one subject, upon which he was not likely to speak—but, none the less, as I had nothing else to do that evening, I assented to his proposition.

I should mention that Mr. Clinton had come into undisputed possession of all that his uncle had. He was well known to be his uncle's only living relative. No will was found. From what Foreclose, Bennion's lawyer, said, it seemed that his client had, for some time past, intended making a will; but, it appeared, he had never got any farther than the intention. Keen man of business and man of the world, as he undoubtedly was, he had died intestate. The result was that Raymond Clinton, whom he had certainly never loved and for whom he had certainly never intended such good fortune, took everything. There was not even a keepsake for Ralph Hardwicke, or for Nina, whom he had loved—yes, both of them. There was nothing to reward Ryan for his long, if not over-faithful, service; not to mention that there was nothing for me, the friend of a life-time—except something which I had secured on my own account, of which no one knew, and which, in the last dread hour which was still to come, I wished with all my heart and soul that I had never seen.

Mr. Clinton had lost no time in entering on the good which, if not the gods, then which something else had given him. He had taken up his abode in Philip Bennion's chambers, and it was in the drawing-room in which Ryan had found his uncle lying dead upon the floor that he received me upon the evening on which I paid him that memorable visit.

I had noticed, during the short time which had elapsed since his uncle's death, that an indefinable change had taken place in the man as I used to know him. In spite of the wonderful improvement which had occurred in his circumstances, he seemed to me to be less at ease than he had been in the uneasiest of his times. Something of his affectation of ultra-fashionable swagger and stupidity had vanished, and he appeared to be more wide-awake, shrewder, and more on the alert than I had ever known him. This change in him struck me very markedly on that particular evening.

The first few moments of our *tête-à-tête* were awkward ones. I had, avowedly, nothing that I wished to say to him, and it appeared, after all, as if he had nothing which he wished to say to me. I sat smoking a cigar; he stood in front of the fire, looking intently at me when I was not looking at him; but directly my glance caught his he looked away in every direction but towards me. I was conscious that this was so, but I did not choose to let him think I noticed it.

At last he broke the silence by putting his fingers into his waistcoat pocket and taking something from it, which he held out to me on the open palm of his hand.

"Is this yours?" he asked.

I recognised it at once. It was a sleeve-link of a some-what curious and costly pattern, one of a pair which I valued not a little.

"It is mine."

"Where did you get it from?"

"I thought it might be yours. Ryan picked it up. He asked me if it was mine. I told him that it was not, but I would inquire of you if it was yours." He paused, and then added, in a tone which was full of meaning, "Ryan picked it up on the floor of this room on the morning on which he found old Ben lying here dead. He picked it up before you came into the room."

As he said this Mr. Clinton looked at me in a manner which I by no means relished.

I was startled—not pleasantly. It was an odd coincidence that I should have worn that sleeve-link, with its fellow, on the night on which I had discussed, with Philip Bennion, "Murder, Considered as One of the Fine Arts." It was odder still that in the morning, when I came to look for it, I should have missed that particular link. How came Ryan to find it on Philip Bennion's drawing-room floor—and before I entered? When the vivid dream which I had dreamed on that fateful night was thus forcibly recalled to my recollection, a cold wave seemed to pass all over me. For a moment I lost my presence of mind.

Through it all I was conscious that Mr. Clinton was regarding me with a fixed intentness of gaze, the meaning of which I could not define. Was it possible that he suspected me? That would be the final straw. To have slain, while fast asleep, my old, if argumentative friend, was bad enough; to be suspected of the crime by Raymond Clinton would be much worse. Better to hang than that.

Finally, but none too soon, he removed his gaze from off my countenance, and, turning to the fire, began to stir the burning coals with the toe of his polished boot. In that attitude he addressed me.

"But it wasn't about the link I wished to speak to you. Glad you've got it back again. Of course I know that you were old Ben's oldest living friend, though I don't think that you ever felt too much friendship for me, and of course I know that, if he had had his way, old Ben would never have died without at least leaving you something which would have served as a memorial of him. It's long odds that he never meant that all the spoils should be mine. So, if you don't mind, I should like you to choose anything which you might fancy, either in this room or anywhere else about the place, and regard it, not as something coming from me, but as a keepsake from old Ben."

Mr. Clinton's little speech took me rather by surprise. I had given him credit neither for such generosity nor for such good taste, not to speak of such right feeling. For the instant I was disposed to give him a hint that if he made a similar offer to Nina Macrae and to Ralph Hardwicke he would do well. But I refrained. I felt that neither he, nor Nina, nor Ralph would thank me. If such an offer was to be made at all, let the original suggestion come from him.

For my own part, I at once made up my mind that I would accept his offer, and that although I already possessed a small relic of his uncle of which he had no notion. I told him so.

"I thank you, Mr. Clinton. I confess to you that I have felt that I should like to have something which belonged to our old friend—something which I might regard as a memorial of our life-long friendship."

"Look round the room, and see if there is anything here which you would care to have."

I did look round the room, and I saw a great many things which I would care to have—care very much to have. I am not myself a collector—that is, I do not make the chief object of my existence the gathering together of a heterogeneous assortment of articles of curiosity—bric-à-brac. But I do know a good thing when I see it, and in that room there were not only things which were good, there were things which, from a money point of view, were priceless—things, for the possession of which, if they were put up to auction, the museums of the world would bid against each other.

After some not inconsiderable dubitation, my glance rested on a cabinet which stood in a corner of the room. I knew it to have been a comparatively recent acquisition of Philip Bennion's. I remembered the burst of triumph with which he had shown it me when it first came home. I had then told myself, and I had, indeed, told him, that I would give something to call it mine. I took it for granted that he had given some fabulous sum for it, though I had no notion of what he really had given. In the matter of the prices which he gave for his treasures he was the most secretive man alive. It was a hobby of his never to tell you where he picked them up, and never to tell you what he paid for them. But I had no doubt that he had paid an enormous sum for that particular cabinet—it was worth it. It was of ebony, perhaps six feet high and some four feet wide. It consisted externally of two cupboards, one above and one below. These cupboards opened in the centre, so that each had two doors. The panels of these doors were inlaid with porcelain plaques, and these plaques were exquisitely painted, notably the plaques on the two doors of the upper cupboard. In the one on the left was the figure of a woman, clad in all the magnificence of sixteenth century costume—probably an Italian fine lady of the period. She was a young and a lovely woman, and, with a smile upon her face, she was holding out, in one hand, what seemed to be a golden key, to a young and handsome cavalier, while with the other she was pointing to a cabinet which was at her side. In the plaque upon the right, cavalier and cabinet both had disappeared, and the woman was alone. She was regarding, this time, with a very curious smile upon her face, her golden key. Although the subject of the picture was enigmatic, if not meaningless, the execution was marvellous. The woman's face, particularly in the second painting, in which she was alone, exercised a singular fascination upon you as you gazed.

I remembered that Bennion had told me that the cabinet had belonged to one of the Medicis. He had added that the interior was beautiful, with a beauty of which the exterior could give you but a faint conception. But, unfortunately, at that time the key had not come home. It required cleaning, or oiling, or something, and was to make its appearance shortly. So that I did not see the cabinet opened, and, as it chanced, I never had seen it opened since.

Rising, I approached the corner in which the cabinet stood.

"I have half a mind, Mr. Clinton, to choose this cabinet, though, at the same time, I have hardly the conscience to deprive you of such a treasure."

"You are welcome to it, if you choose to take it. Only there is one thing—it has no key."

"No key?"

"Ryan says that it has never been opened since the day

that it came home. He says that the key was brought one night—it came by post, Ryan believes—just as old Ben was going out to dinner. Old Ben put it down somewhere, and in the morning, when he came to look for it, he couldn't think where. He and Ryan hunted for it in all directions, but it never has been found since. Ryan says that he believes old Ben put it in his pocket, and lost it while he was out; but old Ben always denied it with fervent protestations."

"So that the cabinet has never been opened?"

"According to Ryan. He says that old Ben was always going to send for a locksmith, but that he never sent."

I said nothing. Clinton might be telling the truth or he might not. I knew him sufficiently well to be aware that it was quite impossible, if one judged merely by appearances, to tell if he was or was not lying. He might be unwilling to part with the cabinet—in which unwillingness he would be perfectly justified—and had invented the story of the lost key—for, in the matter of lies, he was a master of invention—by way of conveying a delicate hint of his disinclination.

If he was unwilling to part with the cabinet—very well! He might keep it. I would choose something else. I was quite clear, in my own mind, that I would have something.

I turned to a number of bronzes which were crowded together on a table which stood against the wall—very fine pieces some of them were. I could see that they had not been touched for some time, for they were covered with dust. I picked them up, one after the other—rather ginger-ly, because of the dust—and examined them, I turned one piece, a curiously-shaped, convoluted vase, upside down, for the purpose of seeing what mark might be underneath. As I did so something rattled in its interior. I shook the vase. Something tumbled out of it on to the table. It was a key of somewhat singular construction, apparently, made of some sort of composition; it looked like gold. It was, possibly, six inches in length. Long and slender in the barrel, the handle was beautifully wrought and finished in a very complicated design. The wards were very intricate, and if they exactly fitted the lock to which they were designed, which one could scarcely doubt, then I should say that that would have been an exceedingly difficult lock to pick. The key, which was unmistakably of foreign workmanship, presented, in its integrity, an excellent example of the locksmith's art.

I picked it up.

"What's this?" I said.

Mr. Clinton came towards me.

"Hallo! A key!"

"Is it the lost key of the cabinet?"

"By Jove! It might be. It looks just like the sort of key a thing like that would have. Where did you find it?"

"It fell out of this vase."

"Fancy if old Ben put it there and forgot all about it. It's just the sort of thing he would have done, and you can see the vase hasn't been touched for months. I've had nothing touched since I've been here. Give it to me; I'll see if it fits. If it does you can have the cabinet and welcome."

I handed him the key. He inserted it in the lock of the cabinet. It went in easily. He commented on the fact.

"George! I believe it is the key. It fits like a glove. Let's see if it will turn."

He was, as I suppose, just about to turn the key when he gave a sort of choking cry, staggered backwards, stood for a moment reeling to and fro, as if in some kind of convulsion, and then fell heavily to the floor.

CHAPTER VI

THE MEDICI CABINET

I WAS so amazed that I stared for a moment at the recumbent figure lying almost at my feet. I expected to see him get up again, or at least to show signs of life. But he lay as if he were dead.

"Mr. Clinton!" I exclaimed, when I had somewhat recovered my presence of mind, and perceived that still he did not move.

He was silent. I leant over him. I was amazed and horrified by the spectacle which he presented. He lay on his back. I could see that his fists were tightly clenched. His lips were slightly parted; a thin line of foam marked their partition. His eyes were half open. I could see that the eye-balls had turned right round in their sockets. His face was all drawn up and puckered, so that he presented the appearance of, as it were, a grinning fiend. I never saw a more unpleasant spectacle.

I perceived at once that the case was serious, that there was something here of which I should not care to accept the responsibility. I summoned Ryan—for Mr. Clinton had, at any rate temporarily, continued his uncle's old servant in his own service.

When Ryan saw Mr. Clinton lying there he was amazed.

"Good Lord!" he cried. "How like the governor he looks."

I myself saw points of similarity between Mr. Clinton's appearance and Philip Bennion's, as we had found him on that never-to-be-forgotten morning. But I also saw points of dissimilarity too. And in any case it was not a moment in which to dwell upon coincidences.

"He is in some sort of a fit," I said. "Let us see what we can do for him." We did see what we could do for him and we did it, both Ryan and I. But in spite of all we could do, I thought at one time that he had followed his uncle—that he had gone after a very brief possession of those good things which his heart so loved.

I was just on the point of summoning medical assistance, and wishing, too, that I had summoned it before, when he gave signs of life—faint signs, but unmistakable signs, despite their faintness.

"Thank goodness!" I exclaimed. "He is not dead!"

He was not dead, but it was some minutes still before he really was alive. And it seemed that his restoration to life was as painful as evidently his temporary departure from it had been. He came back with convulsive shudderings and uncomfortably stertorous breathing.

When he again was fully conscious, sitting up, he looked about him with bewildered eyes.

"What's—what's wrong?"

"That's what I should like to ask you. How are you feeling now?"

"Feeling?" He put his hand up to his brow. "I—I'm feeling dooséd queer."

"You've had some sort of fit. Are you subject to that sort of thing?"

I looked at him attentively as I asked the question. I had never seen such a sudden change take place in a man before. He seemed to have aged ten years in a moment. He looked, to use a figure of speech, like a living corpse. His eyes had sunk deep into his head; his cheeks seemed to have grown thin.

"Fit!" he exclaimed. "Never had such a thing in my life. It was my hand." He held out his right hand in front of him and stared at the palm with a puzzled air, as though he was still not quite himself. "I hurt it. What's that?"

He drew his open palm towards him and pointed at it with the index finger of his left hand. I leant forward to see what it was he pointed at. Nothing was visible except a tiny red spot. It was to that he was pointing.

"It's nothing," I said. "You have pricked yourself, that's all."

"Oh! Think so? Dooséd odd!" He stared about him as if he did not quite know where he was. "Give me some brandy."

We gave him some. We had tried to give him some before between his tightly-clenched teeth. Now he swallowed the better part of half-a-pint neat. It seemed to revive him. He stood upon his feet; he shook himself; he gave a somewhat uncomfortable-looking grin.

"I'm all right. I've only had a touch of the staggers." He turned to Ryan. "You can go." Ryan went. Clinton turned to me. "You needn't look at me like that. I'm all right, I tell you. I only came over a trifle queer. Let's see if that key fits the lock."

He moved towards the cabinet, walking rather shakily. He stood staring at the key, which, when he fell, he had left in the lock, as though even yet he had not recovered complete control of all his faculties.

"Let's see, I was trying if that key fitted, wasn't I? Oh, yes, of course I was. How—how stupid of me to have forgotten. Let's see if it does."

He laid a rather shaky hand upon the handle of the key and, as I again suppose, again endeavoured to turn it. But before he had time to succeed he again gave utterance to that disagreeable choking sound to which he had given utterance before, and again he staggered backwards. This time, however, he turned towards me, and so enabled me to perceive that the muscles of his face were working, as if automatically, in a manner which was absolutely horrible. He seemed to be making a frantic effort to speak, but ere he had opportunity to give utterance to a coherent sound, he again fell backwards with a crash to the floor; and, having fallen, he lay as if he were dead.

This was getting more than a joke. My visit was taking a form for which I had not bargained. I was assisting in a series of little scenes for which I was not by any means prepared. If Mr. Raymond Clinton had a predisposition towards fits, he ought to have warned me that he intended to indulge that predisposition to the full on that particular evening, in which case I should certainly have kept away. I was not sufficiently interested in Mr. Raymond Clinton to care to act as his gratuitous and unskilled medical assistant.

But, as I was there, and the man would indulge himself, I felt that I had better see him out of just this one other. When I had seen him out of it, before I gave him the chance to enjoy another, at least, while I was there—we would see. So again I summoned Ryan, who was unmistakably surprised at this fresh manifestation of his master's peculiar idiosyncrasy, and I did see him out of it—that is, with the assistance of Ryan.

This was not such a lengthy business as the first had been. In fact, it was my opinion that he never had entirely lost consciousness. And while we were still, I suppose, in the middle of the work of resuscitation, Mr. Clinton all at once came to—of his own accord, so to speak—in a manner which amazed me.

He sprang up so suddenly that he all but struck the back

of his head against my nose, which, as I am unusually tender in the immediate neighbourhood of that organ, would have been a nice reward for playing the good Samaritan—sprang right upon his feet. He glanced about him wildly for a moment or two; then, turning to Ryan, he shouted at, rather than spoke to him.

"Get out!" he cried, and pointed to the door.

My first impression was that Mr. Clinton had gone mad, and I was more than half disposed to urge Ryan to stay. But I refrained, and Ryan got out, seemingly not at all unwillingly. Then Mr. Clinton turned to me.

The change in his appearance was really wonderful. A prolonged bout of the severest illness could scarcely have worked a greater. The second attack might not have been so severe as the first had been, but it had left its mark upon him, none the less. He looked worn and haggard, all the life-blood seemed to have left his face. But, in spite of the appearance of pallor, there was about him an appearance of ferocity, too. He seemed to be in a towering rage—he, the man whom I had never judged capable of material discomposure! Fixing his gleaming eyes upon my countenance, he bent forward and said, in a voice which trembled as with passion:

"Do you know what did it?"

"What did what?" I asked.

"Do you know what knocked me down?"

"I have no idea. I imagine that you are in an imperfect state of health."

"Not I! I'm as strong as a horse, and always have been. It was the key!"

"The key!"

He was pointing towards the cabinet. I followed with

my eye the direction in which he pointed; but I had not the faintest notion of what it was he meant.

"The key!" he repeated. "Look at that!" He held out his right hand, palm uppermost. "Just now there was one spot, now there are two."

There certainly were two tiny red spots right in the centre of the palm of his hand. It was equally true that before I had only noticed one.

"But what of that?" I said. "You have pricked yourself again, that's all."

"I have not pricked myself. It was the key which pricked me! I was half conscious of it the first time. I was sure of it the second. Directly I began to turn it, something shot out of the key into my hand."

"Something shot out of the key into your hand?"

"I'll swear to it! It's some infernal contrivance or other. I felt it prick me like a needle, and I believe——" He paused; then added, in a sort of gasp: "By Heaven! Otway, I believe the thing is poisoned!"

I was silent. The truth is, that he had momentarily startled away from me the power of speech. His words filled my mind with a vista of wild imaginings. He moved towards the cabinet. And I thought of the strange tales which are told of the Italian poisoners of the Renaissance, of the days when art was a power in the lands, the days when murder was indeed considered as one of the fine arts; and the ingenuity of the multitudinous contrivances by means of which they conveyed their poisons to their victims; and of a melodramatic legend which I had read somewhere, long ago, of a treasure house, which, when you tried to enter it, and, to enable you to do so, turned the key, which was always left invitingly in the lock, you were struck dead. While such thoughts were traversing my mind, Raymond Clinton, standing before the cabinet, was apostrophising the painted figures on the painted panels. His wild words mingled, appropriately enough, with my wild thoughts.

He addressed himself to the resplendent figure of the smiling woman.

"You see, Otway, she has a key in her hand. George! it is the very spit of the key which you found in the vase, and which I was fool enough to try to turn. She offers it to the man—poor beggar! What's he done to her? She points to the cabinet; upon my soul, it's the double of this. The thing's as plain as porridge!" He pointed to the second picture, in which the woman was alone. "Now, you see, she's done the trick—the man's rubbed out. But she's still got the key in her hand; it was with that she did it! And she's smiling to herself to think that no one will ever know. You Jezebel!" Mr. Clinton actually shook his fist at the painted porcelain. "I wonder how many men you've wiped out with that sweet key of yours before it almost did for me?"

It occurred to me that, after all, he was rather putting the cart before the horse.

"Doesn't it strike you, Mr. Clinton, that you are rather taking things for granted? You have no actual proof that there is anything malevolent in the construction of the key."

He stretched out his hand in front of him.

"No actual proof! What do you call this?"

"Quite so. But suppose we examine the key itself."

"Take care how you touch it, or you will soon have proof enough and to spare."

"I will be careful." I grasped the barrel of the key very cautiously between my finger and thumb. I experienced no difficulty in withdrawing it from the lock. "Do you think there is such a thing as a pair of tweezers anywhere?"

"I shouldn't be surprised. There's a drawer here full of all sorts of things."

The drawer referred to proved to be the kind of drawer which such a collector as Philip Bennion might be expected to have, even in his drawing-room. It contained the tools which might be required for a thousand purposes, and which an enthusiast would always desire to have close at hand. Amongst other things were a pair of tweezers and a daintily-fashioned vice. The vice I screwed, without remorse, and with Mr. Clinton's approbation, to a highly-polished table. In it I fixed the key, wards downwards. Then, with the aid of the pair of tweezers, I essayed to turn the handle.

I met with less resistance even than I expected. At my first slight effort the handle turned quite easily, although independent of the rest of the key, which was held firmly by the vice. At the top of the bar which bound the handle was a little hole, so small that it was only to be noticed by a close inspection. As the handle turned, there shot out of the barrel what looked like a bright steel needle. It passed through the hole in the handle, extending, perhaps, a quarter of an inch beyond it, an extent sufficient to cause a pretty considerable incision in the palm of a man's hand. It appeared for an instant and then vanished, beating a retreat long before I turned the handle back again. I turned the handle two or three times, and each time that curious gleaming little instrument made its instantaneous appearance and departure.

"What devil's game is this!" exclaimed Mr. Clinton.

I could see that the same thought had come to him which had come to me.

If merely turning the handle of that singularly-fashioned

key had had such an effect on Raymond Clinton, what effect might it not have had on Philip Bennion? Supposing he
had tried to turn it on that eventful night? Supposing he had
tried to open that mysterious cabinet? Mr. Clinton's second
attack had been less severe than his first. Possibly the mis-
chievous strength of the thing was weakened by repetition.
Possibly use dulled its powers, and it was only the first user
who proved their full malignancy. If Philip Bennion had endeavoured to open the cabinet, he came before Raymond
Clinton, and he might have found the charming, and, apparently harmless example of the locksmith's art charged as if
with the lightning stroke of death. It would have left upon
him no external mark of what it had done, save, possibly, a
tiny pin-prick on the palm of his hand. And who would have
thought of looking for that? Or who would have thought
anything of it, even if it had been seen?

That the same thought had been simultaneously occupying Mr. Clinton's mind was shown by a remark he made
without my having spoken a word which could have given
him a hint of what I had been thinking.

"It couldn't have been."

"Why not?"

"Ryan tells me, positively, that old Ben lost the key the
night that it came home, and that he never found it afterwards."

"He might have found it on that last night."

"I think not. I don't believe that the vase from which
you unearthed it has been touched for months. And again,
if he had found it, and had put it in the lock, it would still
have been in the lock when—when Ryan discovered him.
Judging from my experience, of which you have been the
witness, he would have been struck down in an instant. He
would surely not have had time to withdraw the key from

the lock, and still less to put it in the vase, which, you will observe, is at some distance from the cabinet. What is more, when Ryan discovered him, he was not near either the cabinet or the vase, but right at the other side of the room."

"That is true." I felt that Mr. Clinton's reasoning—of which, by the way, I had not thought he had been capable—was not without its cogency. "At the same time there are, with your permission, two things which I should like to do. First of all, I should like to submit this key to an authority whose appreciation of its peculiar properties might be juster than yours and mine. Have you any objection?"

"Not the slightest. The sooner you take it away the better I shall be pleased. I always have had an objection to dangerous playthings. I suppose that now you wouldn't care to have the cabinet?"

"On the contrary, I should care to have it more than ever. Its value is enhanced in my eyes by the twofold purpose which, if one may conjecture, it possibly was designed to serve. I would infinitely prefer it, for instance, to one more valuable, which was only a cabinet and nothing more. And there is another thing. I should very much like to know from whom your uncle procured his treasure. I suppose that you have no idea?"

"Not the slightest. He never spoke to me about such things."

"I should like to know, too, if he was acquainted with the peculiar properties of this key. He showed me the cabinet, the outside of it, that is, on the day on which he had it home, but he never hinted at anything of the kind. I remember, indeed, his saying that he did not know what was the subject of the pictures on the panels. If he had been acquainted with the peculiar properties of the key, their subject would have been obvious enough."

"Too obvious!"

Turning, Mr. Clinton again glared at the painted lady.

"One other thing I should like to know. Whether the person from whom he procured the cabinet was acquainted with the peculiar properties of its key."

"He must have been."

"I think it probable. His sending the key home afterwards looks—odd."

"I lay you odds, Otway, that the fellow, whoever he was, before he sent it, charged it with some infernal poison."

"I am bound, myself, to own that it looks curious."

Clinton gave a sudden exclamation.

"I tell you what: I think I have something which will help you to find out where old Ben got the cabinet from." Taking a bunch of keys from his pocket, he opened a drawer in a writing-table. "Here's a sort of diary in which old Ben seems to have entered a lot of odds and ends about his collection. I've only just glanced at it. Perhaps you may be able to find something in it about the cabinet." He took out a leather-covered volume, which was secured by a key. "Here's the key."

He handed me the book and the key.

"Thank you. I think that, as you suggest, I may be able to procure from it some information. And now, Mr. Clinton, I think that I will say good-night."

"One moment." Something curious in his tone caused me to glance at him. "I have a word or two which I wish to say to you."

He stood for some seconds looking at me attentively, while I waited for him to speak. Then he crossed the room.

"I wonder where that Ryan is? I have not the highest opinion of that gentleman." He opened the three doors which the room possessed, moving from one to the other, and looked outside. "He doesn't seem to be anywhere about. I don't want to have him listening. But this room is such a thundering large one, that I don't think he'll be much wiser, even if he has a weakness for the keyhole."

CHAPTER VII

MR. CLINTON'S STATEMENT

RETURNING to the fireplace, Mr. Clinton took up his position with his back to it. After his behaviour with regard to the doors, I was prepared for some peculiar, and probably characteristic, observation. But I was not prepared for what he actually did say, nor did I understand what he meant when he said it.

"Mr. Otway"—he cleared his throat, as if he found some difficulty in saying what he had to say. I noticed, too, that he fidgeted from foot to foot—"I suppose that you and I are in the same boat together?"

"I beg your pardon?"

"I say that as you and I are in the same boat together, we may as well be plain with one another."

"I am afraid that I do not understand you."

"Don't you?" Something very like a savage gleam came into his eyes. "Then you very soon shall. I'm sick of this." The man whom I had always known in his most insolent and rascally moods to be as cool as a cucumber, seemed, to-night, to have entirely changed his nature. He spoke quite ferociously. "I'm a man who likes to know just where I am standing, and I've never had a moment's peace of mind since—since old Ben died. So perhaps you'll be so good as to tell me, straight out, if you saw me that night."

"If I—what?"

"If you saw me that night. I speak plainly enough, and you know very well what I mean."

"I assure you that you flatter my perspicuity. I have not the most distant comprehension of your meaning."

"George! Otway, I believe you're a cleverer man than I thought you were." Mr. Clinton's equivocal compliment seemed to be genuinely meant; though what had prompted it was more than I could guess. "I'll be straight with you, anyhow. Therefore, Mr. Otway, I beg to inform you that I did see you."

"You saw me—when?" As I saw that he smiled I added: "You may smile, Mr. Clinton, but I am still so dull as not to understand you. When did you see me? And what was the peculiarity of the circumstances that you should wish to recall them to me now?"

He came and laid his hand upon my arm, and dropped his voice almost to a whisper—by no means a friendly whisper.

"Do you mean to tell me that you don't know that I saw you on the night on which old Ben—died?"

I stared at him. I perceived that his words conveyed some hidden and some unpleasant meaning, which, however, still I did not catch.

"You saw me on the night on which your uncle died. Well, what then?"

"What then? You ask what then? What is your little game? Do you think I'm going to let you hold that little card, and play it, one day when it suits you, with a view to plunder?"

I shook his hand from off my arm.

"Mr. Clinton, you speak in riddles. Will you be so good as to tell me in plain English, sufficiently plain to be suited to my limited comprehension, precisely what it is you mean?"

He came still closer. His pallid face—pallid from the effects of the two attacks from which he had recently recovered—became still more pallid. He clutched my arm with convulsive force. And he said, as if inspired with sudden, ungovernable rage:

"Otway, I believe you killed him!"

"Killed him! I? Killed who!"

"You killed old Ben! Own it, you hound, or, as I'm alive, I'll shake the life light out of you."

He did shake the life half out of me. He took me by the shoulders and shook me as if I were a rat. He was a young man, and I was an old one. And I was so amazed at his extraordinary language, and such was the suddenness of his attack, that the capacity to offer even the smallest resistance was quite gone from me. He shook me, I say, as if I had been a rat; and when he had had, as I presume, enough of shaking me—and I had had more than enough of being shaken—he threw me from him, and hurled me backwards with so much violence that I fell headlong to the floor.

It was several seconds before I recovered myself sufficiently to resume a perpendicular position, and then I felt as if all my bones had become unjointed.

"Mr. Clinton, you are either a cowardly scoundrel or a raving madman."

He advanced towards me again. I retired. I thought it better.

"Tell me what you were doing in here at three o'clock in the morning?"

"In here at three o'clock in the morning—I? Mr. Clinton, I am beginning to be strongly of opinion that something has happened, you best know what, to unhinge what little mind you ever had. I never remember to have been in this room at three o'clock in the morning in all my life."

He threw up his hands to the ceiling.

"This man out Tartuffes Tartuffe! Have you forgotten— have you so poor a memory, you king of hypocrites?—that I saw you come out of your room and come in here? When you came in here the room was lighted; when you went out of it it was all in darkness. Possibly you felt that for the deed which you had done darkness was more appropriate than light; but what it was you did is known only to God, and to old Ben, and to you."

I did not sit—I sank down into a chair. A cold sweat broke out all over me. My dream! The vivid recollection I had had of putting out the electric light! I gasped rather than spoke:

"You saw me come in here!" I made an effort to recover myself. "May I ask, Mr. Clinton, what you were doing here at that hour to see me?"

"I will tell you. I was a villain; but the thought of it all has so nearly driven me mad that I will make a clean breast of it, even if it spoils me. I was stony; I was in an awful hole. I had asked old Ben for coin, but he wouldn't part. But coin I was bound to have, or I should come to frightful grief, safe as houses. I made up my mind that I would get coin somehow. I knew that old Ben kept a lot in a drawer in the writing-table here—he was a queer stick about that sort of thing—and I—I happened to have a key which would fit that drawer. I made up my mind I would use that key. I stole into the chambers at three o'clock in the morning—never mind how I got in, I did get in—and I had got as far as outside this room when I heard a noise. I slunk into the little alcove which is between the door and the wall, and I saw the door of your room opened, and I saw you come out. You came straight in here, and as you came in here, I could see that the room was lighted. That was more than I had bargained for. I knew that old Ben was an early bird, and I had taken it for granted that he would have gone to roost long before that time. I don't know how long you were in there, but it seemed to me to be hours; but under circumstances such as mine were time don't go quickly. When you came out I could see that the room was all in darkness. As you came out you turned right round, and you saw me. I was never in such a state in my life. I went all of a heap. For the life of me I didn't know what to say or do. I just mumbled 'Mr. Otway,' but you said nothing. You stared at me for a good half minute, and then you turned right round and walked straight into your own room. I saw that I was in for it, because I knew that you were no friend of mine, and that you'd be sure to tell old Ben that you'd seen me hanging about his room, like an area thief, at three o'clock in the morning. So I told myself that I might as well be hung for a sheep as a lamb. It seemed to me that it was a case of smash either way, and as I felt sure that old Ben wouldn't prosecute if the worst came to the worst, and as I knew that—that some one else would if I couldn't lay my hands upon some coin, I made up my mind to see the thing through and go for the gloves. I waited till I thought old Ben would be safe to have gone to bed, and then I tried the door. I had brought a pass key, but, to my surprise, I found that it was open. When I had got inside, and had shut the door behind me, I struck a match, for it was so dark that I couldn't see my nose before my face. As I did so, I saw—my God! shall I ever forget it?—I saw old Ben lying on the floor in front of me. I was so taken aback that I let the match go out, and, upon my soul, I could hear my own heart beating against my ribs. I waited. There was not a sound. I struck another match—it was as much as I could do, I was trembling so—and I went and looked at old Ben. I shall never forget the feelings with which I saw that he was dead, not if I live to be a hundred. You hound!"

Mr. Clinton paused in his narrative to shake his fist at me.

"If I had not been the greatest cur that ever breathed

I should have given the alarm and set the dogs at you at once. But I was so taken aback, and I was myself so conscience-stricken, that I gave way to panic, and, there and then, I made a bolt of it, without ever thinking of the coin which I'd come after. But in the morning I couldn't keep away, and when I came and saw you and Ryan looking at old Ben, and saw the way in which you carried it off, I felt funny. I thought that your game was that if I didn't give you away, you wouldn't give me. But since then I haven't been able to make you out. So I have resolved that I will come to an understanding with you as to what the position really is. You will be so good as to tell me before you leave this room what you did to old Ben, because, Mr. Otway, I mean to know."

I am not going to attempt to describe the emotions with which I listened to Mr. Clinton's statement, because, in that direction, I have no skill. Of one thing, as he went on, I became convinced, that he was telling the truth according to his rights. And, regarded from the most charitable point of view, a disgraceful truth it was.

"Mr. Clinton," I said, when, after an interval of silence, I had regained sufficient mastery of myself to enable me to speak, "whatever I did, I did it in a dream."

"In a dream! You—you A1 liar! Look here, Mr. Otway, it's no good of your trying that line with me. I assure you I'm not the fool you evidently take me for—upon my honour!"

"Mr. Clinton, when you saw me I was walking in my sleep."

"Walker!"

"Have you never heard that I am a somnambulist? Among my acquaintances it is a matter of common notoriety."

He reflected for a moment, or he appeared to reflect.

"I have heard something about it. But don't ask me to believe that, in a fit of somnambulism, you killed old Ben. It would be too thin, it really would."

"I have given careful attention to what you had to say. I must ask you to give equally careful attention to what I have to say. And I may state at once, by way of preface, and since frankness is the order of the day, that I have, on my part, entertained the strongest suspicions that it was you who killed your uncle."

Mr. Clinton stared.

"I! That's good! Really, Mr. Otway, in your way you are a perfect gem."

"I will be as frank with you as you have been with me. I have believed from the first that a crime has been committed. My sole desire is to establish the truth. If Philip Bennion was your uncle, he was my lifelong friend. I will leave no stone unturned till the crime has been brought to light, and the criminal to book. If you will hear me out, you will understand—what you profess to wish to understand—what the position really is."

Mr. Clinton smiled. I could see that he intended to take anything I might say with a liberal allowance of salt. But, in spite of his ostentatious predisposition to incredulity, I said my say.

"On the night on which your uncle—died, he had been paying me a visit. We had been talking—in the light of after events it seems a very strange and a very notable coincidence—on murder, considered as one of the fine arts. Your uncle had some curious opinions on that subject, and he expressed them, as he was wont to do, with sufficient warmth. After he had left me, I remained thinking of the matter of our conversation. And in the night I dreamed."

I paused, and Mr. Clinton smiled. I refused to allow his smile to provoke from me any signs of irritation.

"I dreamed that I got out of bed and came into his room—this room. Here there occurred, so far as my recollection serves me, a hiatus in my dream. I am not clear as to what, in my dream, happened immediately on my entrance. But I have a hazy recollection of touching your uncle, and saying, 'I will show you the "Artist in Murder."' The phrase, 'Artist in Murder,' we had used frequently in our conversation. I am not clear if he fell when I touched him, or if he had fallen before I touched him. But I have a clear recollection of looking down upon him as he lay, and then of moving two or three paces from him, and putting out the electric light. You may imagine my feelings when, with that dream still vividly in my mind, in the morning I knelt by your uncle's corpse. Until this evening I have been unable to satisfy myself as to whether there was any reality in what I had supposed to be a dream. But, after your spontaneously offered explanation, I cannot doubt that I actually did what I dreamed of doing. That, however, I had a hand in Philip Bennion's death I never did believe, and I believe it still less after our experience with the cabinet, and its peculiarly constructed key."

Mr. Clinton looked at me as if he sought to read my inmost soul. I could see that my words had impressed him, although he might not choose to own it.

"What made you entertain that flattering supposition that it was I who put old Ben away?"

I hesitated, and then spoke frankly.

"Mr. Clinton, I believe that you are aware that I have not had the highest opinion of your moral character. I have been made too intimately acquainted with certain details of your career. I was aware that you were pressed for money.

I was aware that your uncle had refused you further aid. There, at least, was motive."

He laughed a little hollowly.

"Did you see me in that wonderful dream of yours? You looked at me hard enough. Good Lord, how you stared!"

"I did not see you. I assure you that if I had, I should have told you so pretty plainly, sir."

"If your conscience was so clear, why did you not tell this story of yours at the inquest?"

"What was I to tell? That I had dreamed? If you had told me before what you have told me now, I should have taken steps to have both you and myself called as witnesses."

He did not seem altogether to relish the suggestion. He looked down at his toes, then glanced up again at me.

"Supposing that you did kill old Ben, in a state of somnambulism—and, on your own showing, you don't know that you didn't—what would they do to you?"

"I have not the faintest notion. I promise you this. I will make it my first and chiefest business to throw light upon the subject. And you, of course, are free to take what steps you please. And should I discover any further cause to suppose that it was I who killed my friend, I will at once place the case in the hands of the proper authorities. But I do not believe that from me he received the slightest injury—not even when I was, so to speak, in the delirium of sleep. He was my oldest and my closest friend. We had differed on many subjects and on many occasions. But we understood each other, and we never quarrelled. I owed him no grudge. I felt towards him no resentment—nothing but goodwill. I have been afflicted from childhood with the disease of sleep-walking. But I cannot believe that, even in what I will call the paroxysms of my disease, I would, or could, imbue my unconscious hands with the life-blood of my friend."

CHAPTER VIII

IN SEARCH OF RICHARD GENT

WHEN I returned to my own apartments, I examined the volume which Mr. Clinton had taken from the drawer in his uncle's writing-table. I felt bound to do something which would divert my mind from the thoughts and the doubts which pressed upon it. I had never imagined that my interview with Raymond Clinton would have furnished me with such ample food for meditation. I was almost unmanned by the revelation that, after all, I had not dreamed, but that I actually had gone in to Philip Bennion. In spite of my protestations to Mr. Clinton there was still the awful question asking of my heart: Had I killed my friend? And this despite the fact that I was conscious that my doubts of Clinton had by no means disappeared.

I turned, as I have said, to the book with which Mr. Clinton had entrusted me, in the hope of finding in its pages the wherewithal to divert my attention from too personal and too sombre a theme. I found sufficient cause for diversion, of one kind, if not of another.

It was, as Mr. Clinton had suggested, a kind of diary. Philip Bennion appeared to have used it for a variety of purposes—some of which purposes not a little astonished me. There was, so far as I could judge from a cursory examination, no sort of order or arrangement about the book. Bennion seemed to have jotted down, as the fancy took him, here a memorandum of the occurrences of the day, there a reflection, so to speak, upon men and manners.

But the book principally dealt with his collection, and that in rather a peculiar way. There would be an entry of the purchase of a particular specimen, of how much he had paid for it, from whom he had purchased it. And then would follow comments upon the price, the purchaser, the purchase itself. And I was amused to note how frankly he had dealt, in his private and particular memorandum-book, with the demerits of the additions which he had made to his collection.

As thus—he appears to have been in Paris at the time the entry was made—"June 23.— Bought ivory snuff-box, a hundred francs, from Foulard, 27, Rue de Becq. Doubtful acquisition. Foulard says box belonged to a Marquis de Filoselle, was painted for him by one of the ladies of the Court, and was found on the Marquis's body after he had been guillotined. Doubt it. However, not bad box; has got a history—if a lying one! Foulard wanted two hundred francs, so was ass enough to give him a hundred."

I happened to remember the snuff-box to which this entry evidently alluded. Bennion had dilated for an hour on its romantic history, to the literal and particular truth of which he had been prepared to swear. These collectors! I always had entertained suspicions as to the authenticity of Philip Bennion's most genuine antiques. The expression of them had, more than once, almost driven him mad. And now it was shown that he had entertained them all the time himself. I am forced to admit that I had never suspected him of such duplicity as that.

It was some time before I lighted on any allusion to that mysterious cabinet. At last, however, I came to what I was looking for. It was under a date which was not yet six months old.

"Bought, Italian cabinet, beginning of sixteenth century, a hundred guineas, from Richard Gent, No.—, Brompton Road. The man's a fool! The cabinet would not have been dear at fifty times the price. It is as fine an example of the period as I ever saw. Should say it is as fine an example as there is extant. Four paintings on four front panels, marvellously done! Don't know where Gent got it from; newcomer, never heard of him before. Should say he stole it. Even then the man's a fool to take a hundred, and I gave him what he asked. Key wanted cleaning or something—couldn't quite make out what—but coming home."

That was the cabinet, and that was the key! My own recollection served me as to the date. It only required a slight effort of memory to recall that it must have been about that period that Philip Bennion had called me in, in triumph, to show me his new purchase.

The more I looked at that entry in Philip Bennion's diary, the less I liked it, the darker were the suspicions which shadowed my mind. There was more than one point about it which struck me disagreeably.

There was the small price, so small as to cause Bennion to suggest, evidently not altogether in jest, that the man must have stolen it to enable him to sell it at such a price. My own limited knowledge made me aware that to ask only a hundred guineas for such a cabinet as that was little else than an absurdity. As Bennion himself observed, fifty times the sum would have been nearer the mark. What could have induced a dealer, a man whose business it is to make himself acquainted with the value of his wares, and who not seldom places on them a higher value than his customers, to have parted with what must almost certainly have been the finest example in his stock at a price so obviously disproportioned to its intrinsic worth?

I wondered!

Then, again, there was the fact, which Bennion had noted, of the key not having been sent home with the cabinet. Why had that eccentric dealer in bric-à-brac, Mr. Richard Gent, retained it? What had been the exact nature of the "cleaning" process to which it had been subjected? I felt that I should very much like to know. And, if putting a civil question to Mr. Richard Gent would suffice to elicit the information, I would know in the morning. Philip Bennion had evidently not altogether understood the matter. I understood it less than he had done.

Another curious feature which struck me about this curious transaction was the fact that, according to Philip Bennion's statement, Richard Gent was a "new-comer." I suppose there never lived a man who was better acquainted with the dealers in bric-à-brac than Philip Bennion had been. He knew something about them all personally, and not only by repute. There was scarcely a day of his life, a large part of which he had not spent in routing out the contents of some dealer's shop or other. I verily believe that he knew what they had almost as well as they did themselves. And when he made a note of the fact that Richard Gent was a "new-comer, never heard of him," it meant much.

It was certainly, as I have remarked, another curious feature in the history of that curious transaction that Philip Bennion should have purchased that remarkable cabinet, with its remarkable key, from a man who had been a perfect stranger to him, and of whom he had never even heard before.

I resolved that the next day I would make it my business to look up Mr. Richard Gent upon my own account.

The next morning, so soon as I had breakfasted, I packed up the dainty key of that dainty cabinet, enclosed it in a little box, and addressed it to Mr. Lewis Cowan, that world-famed authority on the nature and properties of poisons. I wrote a letter describing, to the best of my ability and so far as I knew them, the peculiarities of that peculiar key, and asking him to let me know whether it was, or was not, charged with poisonous matter, and, if so, what was the character of the poison, and what were the results which it would be likely to have upon any one with whom it came actively into contact.

This letter—which I had marked "Very urgent"—and the package I left in person at Mr. Lewis Cowan's door. And having done so, I hied me to what I hoped would be a satisfactory little interview with Mr. Richard Gent.

In that memorandum of purchase which he had entered in his note-book, Philip Bennion had exactly stated the street, and the number of the street, in which Mr. Richard Gent's establishment was to be found—number so-and-so, Brompton Road. I was, therefore, not prepared to experience any difficulty in finding it. Brompton Road is a sufficiently well-known thoroughfare. I had always been given to understand that it was not one in which a man could take a shop for a month or two and then vacate it, but it appeared that that was exactly what Mr. Richard Gent had done.

The number to which Philip Bennion had so particularly referred was empty—both the house and the shop. For there was a shop, though it was but a little one. It was on the right-hand side of the street, going down from Knightsbridge, just above where the pavement was widest—and it is wide just there. It was a very little shop, with a little, old-fashioned window. When I reached it the only thing to be seen in the window was a bill—"This Shop to Let. Apply"—to the agents. There was no sign about the place of recent tenancy. To my eyes it looked dirty and neglected, as if it had been empty for months; not at all the sort of shop which, if I were in a speculative frame of mind,

I should care to take. Nor was there anything to inform one as to what had been the nature of the business which therein had last been carried on. So far as I could see, by dint of staring through the grimy little window, the interior was destitute of fittings. Moreover, there was no name over the shop-front, nor was there anything of any sort which went to show what the last tenant had been.

I felt, as I stood in front of that dingy little excuse for a shop, that the mystery of that cabinet, and of its key, was likely, so far as Mr. Richard Gent was concerned, to remain a mystery. I concluded that, at any rate, on that morning, I should not be able to put to him those few questions which I should so very much have liked to have put, and which, indeed, I had come there specially to put.

I looked to see what the shops were which were on either side of the empty one. On the right was a confectioner's. The window of the shop on the left was shaded by a high wire blind, on the centre of which was inscribed in large gold letters, surmounted by the Royal arms, a name—"Vose." I suspected that it was a tailor's, and a high-class tailor's too. The shop looked as though it were an old-established one. If I was to obtain any information about the departed Mr. Richard Gent, it was probable that I should obtain it there.

So I entered Mr. Vose's shop.

I was right in my conjecture—it was a tailor's. A tall, portly individual came forward. I inquired of him for Mr. Vose. He informed me that he was that gentleman. Taking out my card-case I gave him my card.

"I am Mr. Otway, of Piccadilly Mansions. I merely wish to ask you if you can tell me anything about a Mr. Richard Gent, who, last July, occupied the shop next door?"

Mr. Vose looked at me, then he looked at my card. Then he said, speaking with a slight Teutonic accent:

"It was last July that Mr. Gent went away."

"Last July? Are you sure?"

"I am very sure. It was the thirteenth of July. That happens to be my birthday, and that causes me to remember it."

I was startled. The thirteenth of July! Philip Bennion had only bought the cabinet, according to the entry in his diary, on the tenth of July. Three days afterwards Mr. Gent had gone away. Not improbably the thirteenth was the day on which he had returned the key.

Seeing that I remained silent, Mr. Vose went on to make a further observation which did not tend to diminish my bewilderment.

"Mr. Gent was only there five weeks—not five weeks, I think, not quite."

"Not five weeks? Indeed! I was under the impression that he had been there much longer than five weeks. The Mr. Gent I refer to was a dealer in bric-à-brac."

"That is so—that is the man. I only learnt his name, Mr. Gent, through the postman; but there is no doubt that it is the same man." Mr. Vose looked again at my card, seemed to reflect a moment, and then asked me a question which nearly took my breath away: "Pardon me, Mr. Otway, but are you the gentleman who purchased the Medici cabinet?"

"The Medici cabinet! May I ask, Mr. Vose, what you know about the cabinet?"

Mr. Vose shrugged his shoulders.

"Ah, it is very little that I know—not so much as I would like to know, by a great deal. You must know, Mr. Otway, that I, too, am a collector"—Mr. Vose apparently had a trick of taking things a good deal for granted—"in my little way, of course. And when the shop next door was opened, I dropped in, in a neighbourly way, to see if the new man had anything which might take my fancy. There was a little rubbish, not much, for the shop was almost empty—and it does not hold much, as you can see. At the back there was something which was covered over with a cloth. I had the shop to myself, because no one seemed to have heard me come in, so I lifted up the cloth to see what it was. I assure you, after the rubbish I had seen, the whole lot of which was not worth a five-pound note, I never was so astonished in my life. It was the finest sixteenth century Italian cabinet, I should think, there is in the world. I never saw anything finer, not in a museum nor anywhere. The panels were painted—I know a little of painting; I never saw anything more fine. I was wondering how such a cabinet as that could have got into that dog-hole of a place, when Mr. Gent came in. He was quite in a temper. He seemed to think that I had taken a liberty in lifting the cloth. I told him who I was, that I was his neighbour, and a collector, and so on, and I asked him how much he wanted for his cabinet. He hummed and he hahed. I could scarcely get him to state a price at all. But at last he said that he would not take less than five thousand guineas, and it struck me, from his tone, that he would not care to sell it even for that."

Five thousand guineas! In his memorandum Philip Bennion had declared that the cabinet was worth fifty times what he had given for it. Here were his hundred guineas multiplied by fifty.

Mr. Vose went on. He had waxed enthusiastic while speaking of the beauties of the cabinet.

"Five thousand guineas for a cabinet was not in my line—not quite, you may believe. But day after day I dropped in next door to ask Mr. Gent if he would not take a little less—a little less. But no, he would not bate a single farthing. He was inclined to raise his figures rather than to lower them. And I do believe that, in the end, I would have bought it, for, after all, it would not have been a bad investment for my money. Only one day, when I dropped in, he told me he had sold it. It had gone."

"Sold it? Did he tell you to whom?"

"No, he did not tell me that. But I asked him how much he had got for it. He looked at me, and he smiled, and he said he had got his price."

"His price? Did he say that he had got five thousand guineas?"

"He named no sum exactly; but he gave me the impression that he had got more than five thousand guineas."

More than five thousand guineas! Could Philip Bennion's entry in his diary of the sum which he had given for the cabinet have been deliberately false? I began to wonder if Mr. Richard Gent had been an even greater fool than his customer had imagined him to be. What was the mystery?

Mr. Vose seemed to be a communicative sort of person. I put to him another question.

"What kind of a man was this Mr. Gent? I mean, what kind of a man was he to look at?"

Mr. Vose half closed his eyes, as if the better to form a mental picture.

"He was a slight, short, pretty young man, with an olive skin, straight black hair, and a big, black moustache. He had a sulky, disagreeable manner, not at all the sort of manner which helps a man who wants to find a customer. I will say this for him, that he never tried to make a customer of me. I don't know why, but he always seemed to me as if he would like to kick me out into the street, and would rather see me hanged than sell to me his precious cabinet. He called himself Gent, and he spoke English very well indeed, as well, for instance, as I do; but for all that, unless I am mistaken, he was an Italian born and bred."

"Is it an impertinence on my part to ask, Mr. Vose, what price you offered for the cabinet?"

"I do not mind telling you, not in the least. I offered three thousand guineas, and I would give three thousand guineas now, this moment, to any gentleman who desired to sell it."

Mr. Vose looked at me as if he more than half suspected that I might be such a gentleman. I am free to confess that I was conscious of a feeling of gratification as I became aware that I had got something out of Raymond Clinton which was actually worth three thousand guineas. I had never expected to receive, from such a quarter, such a windfall. Philip Bennion himself could scarcely have acknowledged our friendship more handsomely, even if he had lived to make his will. Indeed, I doubted very much if he would ever have enriched me to the extent of three thousand guineas.

"One more question I would ask you, Mr. Vose. Did you notice, or did Mr. Gent point out to you, any peculiarity about the cabinet?"

"Peculiarity!" Mr. Vose again became enthusiastic. "I noticed this striking peculiarity about it, that it was the finest cabinet I ever saw, the very finest—and there was no need to point that out to me."

I smiled. Mr. Vose had misunderstood my meaning.

"That was hardly what I meant. I meant to ask if you noticed any peculiarity in the mechanical construction of the cabinet. When you saw it was it locked?"

"No, I do not think that it was locked—I am sure that it was not. I remember, quite well, that Mr. Gent used to throw the doors open with his hands that I might look at the interior. Ah, what an interior—it was superb!"

"How often did you see it, Mr. Vose?"

"As often as Mr. Gent would let me, which was not often. He would never let me look at it without a fuss, as if he wished to let me see as little of it as he possibly could."

I made a mental note of his words and wondered.

"Did you ever minutely examine it?"

"Pretty minutely."

"And you never saw anything peculiar in its mechanical construction?"

"Nothing."

"And Mr. Gent never hinted at anything of the kind?"

"Not a word. Why? Has anything been found? A secret drawer, or what is it? In most of these cabinets there are secret drawers."

I let Mr. Vose's question go unanswered.

"Did you ever notice a key to it?"

He reflected.

"I do not think I did. Has the key been lost?"

"Not that I am aware of. I only wondered."

I paused, trying to think if there was any other question which it might be desirable to ask. Mr. Vose seemed to be trying to read my countenance. He dropped his voice to a confidential whisper.

"Mr. Otway, if the gentleman who purchased the Medici cabinet is thinking of selling it, I would entreat it as a favour that I should be allowed to make an offer. I think it very possible that he and I might come to terms."

"I think, Mr. Vose, that I may venture to promise that if the cabinet does come into the open market, the fact shall be mentioned to you. By the way, didn't it strike you as being rather singular that Mr. Gent should have given up the occupation of his shop after so short a tenancy?"

"Well, I was surprised at first, because I did not know that he was going, and when I came to business in the morning he was gone. But, afterwards I was not surprised. All the time I believed he had come to England only to sell the Medici cabinet—the truth is he had nothing else to sell—and when he sold it, and three days afterwards was gone, I knew that I was right."

For my part I, too, was beginning to believe that Mr. Gent had only taken the shop to enable him to sell the cabinet. But why had he asked, and even been disinclined to accept, five thousand guineas from Mr. Vose, and snatched at a hundred from Philip Bennion?

The thing was a riddle.

CHAPTER IX

NINA VISITS ME AGAIN

On the afternoon of that day I received a visit from Miss Macrae. There was about her, as she came in, an air of repressed excitement—the air of a person who not only has something to tell, but who burns to tell it. She looked, I thought, prettier than ever; and tall, willowy Nina had been always pretty. There was an alertness in her step and in her manner, a light in her eyes, a flush upon her cheeks, a smile about her lips; which things were, to her, an added charm.

She stood at the door, holding the handle in her hand, looking at me with a roguish smile. After the thoughts which had been occupying my mind of late, to the exclusion of all others, that smile came like a ray of sunshine.

"Guardian!"

Crossing the room she laid her two gloved hands upon my shoulders and stooped to kiss me, then looked at me, with merry glances, from under the broad brim of a bewitching hat.

"Ward!"

She laughed, as if my mild *tu quoque* had been intended for a jest. As she continued to regard me, a slight shadow flitted across her face.

"What is the matter with you? What have you been doing, you bad man? Do you know that you look worried?"

I deemed it more than possible. It would have been strange if I had not looked worried. But I did not choose to tell her so.

"Youth and age, my dear, youth and age. When you attain to my years of wisdom—if you ever become so wise—

you will learn that a certain gravity of feature is befitting."

I do not think that my evasion altogether contented her, but she let my words pass muster. She went and stood before the fire, and began to play with the things upon the mantelshelf. A fine picture of English maidenhood. She was like sunshine in the room. I was glad to have her there.

"Guardian!" As she spoke she was looking down at the dancing flames. Her lips were parted in a smile; in her eyes there was a smile as well. "I have something which I wish to tell you."

"You do not say so. It is impossible."

She glanced up quickly.

"What do you mean?" She flushed. "Guardian, have you guessed?"

Calm, self-possessed Miss Nina all at once was crimson. "Red as a rose was she." It became her very well, indeed, that roseate hue.

"Guessed? My dear, what is there I could guess!"

But I fancy that she saw a twinkle in my eyes. For, suddenly, she knelt down upon the rug, and put her elbows on my knees, and looked me closely in the face. After all, old age has certain privileges which are not, upon the whole, unpleasant. The saucy, yet tender, familiarity with which young and even pretty women seldom hesitate to treat one, is not among the least of them.

"Mr. Otway! You wicked man!"

What had I done that I was accused of wickedness?

"Miss Macrae! In what have I sinned?"

"You know all about it, you know you do."

"I? My dear young lady, I know nothing. I never did know anything; I never shall."

She covered her eyes with her gloved hands.

"Guardian, he has told me that he loves me."

I pretended to be amazed.

"He! Good Heavens! Who?"

"You know very well, sir. Ralph."

With what an air of reverential rapture she spoke the name. It had its sweet, as well as its humorous side. Dear lady, was there never a time when you pronounced a name like that? I hope, for your own sake, that it comes from your lips as tenderly to-day.

"Ralph? Is it possible that you mean Ralph Hardwicke?"

She took her hands away. She looked at me with gleaming eyes.

"Of course I mean Ralph Hardwicke. Guardian, aren't you glad?"

"In such a case as this, my dear, I fancy that it is not my feelings which are of primary importance, but yours."

"You know very well what I mean. May I?"

"May you what? May you give him permission to tell you that he loves you? I think it possible that your permission might not be asked. From what I know of Mr. Hardwicke, I fancy—it may be only fancy, but there it is—but I fancy that if he had made up his mind to tell you that he loved you, he would tell you, with your permission or without."

"I think he would." She looked down, pretending to pick up imaginary pieces of cotton from my trouser knees. "He never asked my permission, I assure you. He quite frightened me, indeed."

"Beware, young lady, of hypocrisy—that besetting sin of women and of girls."

"He did frighten me, I declare it's true." She smiled her sauciest smile. "I don't say that it was a disagreeable kind of fright, you know."

"Young lady, I am, as you are aware, an old man, and

in my way an observer of human nature. I have often wondered what are the sensations of a young woman when a young man first tells her that he loves her. If you will kindly favour me with an analytical account of yours I will enter it, for purposes of future reference, in my commonplace book."

As she looked at me, both laughter and defiance were in her eyes.

"Would you like me to favour you with a full and particular account just now?"

"At your pleasure and at your leisure. At the same time, I should like to be informed if you were favouring me with an account of your sensations when the first man first told you that he loved you. In these matters one likes to have all available data."

"It is neither the second nor the third man, but it will be the last."

"The last? How so?"

"How so? Just as though you didn't know! Those other men said that they loved me. This time I know that I love him."

"This is—really, this is—ought I to say, this is deplorable?"

"I can tell you that you had better not. You dare! Guardian!" Stretching out her arms, she again laid her hands upon my shoulders. She became very much in earnest all at once. "Say that I may be his wife!"

"Is it for me to say, or for you?"

"Do not laugh at me—not now." A perceptible change took place in the tone of her voice. I thought it was rather an odd change, too. "You know, or perhaps you don't know, but it is a fact, that the one subject on which Mr. Bennion and I didn't quite agree was this." She paused. When she resumed, in her voice there was an obvious tremor. "Of course, Ralph had never said anything to me. At least, nothing particular; but I suppose that Mr. Bennion saw I liked him, because he went out of his way to warn me that I was to have as little to do with Ralph as I possibly could. I have always believed that he spoke to Ralph, too, because, just before that time, Ralph went away."

I was surprised. I had supposed that it would have been the chief desire of Philip Bennion's life that these two should come together. Certainly I had never seen anything in him which would have led me to think the contrary. He was not a demonstrative man, few men less so, but I knew that they had both been to him as his children. They were the dearest things he had in the world. I verily believe that they were even dearer to him than his collection! And I had always imagined, and had always supposed that I had reason to believe, that the crowning object of his life would be attained when he saw them together as man and wife.

And yet I was not so surprised as I should have been if she had spoken to me, for instance, the day before. Because last night, in glancing through Philip Bennion's diary, I had lighted on some words which seemed to suggest that some such objection as Nina referred to had all the time existed in his mind. Nina's words seemed to confirm what I had only glanced at, and had certainly not entirely understood.

Nina was waiting for me to speak.

"Did he ever give any reason why he wished you to keep apart from Ralph?"

"Not the slightest. He was quite disagreeable. I thought him most unkind."

"Are you sure you did not misunderstand him? It was always my idea that nothing would have given him greater pleasure than to see you two together." She looked down, then, a moment after, looked up again with a burning blush.

"So I thought. Why should I conceal it from you? You won't think any the worse of me." She clasped her hands gently about my own. "So I thought, until he told me the contrary. It was quite impossible to misunderstand him; he told me so over and over again. And when he wasn't speaking I felt that he was watching me. I believe he knew every time I spoke to Ralph, and almost what I said to him. I feel sure that he spoke to Ralph and sent him abroad, because I feel certain, never mind why, but I do feel certain," and again Miss Nina blushed—she was in a blushing mood that day—"that Ralph would never have gone if it hadn't been for him."

I pondered the young lady's words, as taking my ease in my great armchair, with her kneeling on the rug in front of me, I sat and watched her radiant face. I reflected that there are none so blind as those who won't see, and that, after all, it is not always the looker-on who sees most of the game. All this had been going on before my eyes—this little comedy of the stern guardian and the unwilling ward, and I, who fancied myself omniscient, had seen nothing at all.

"What reasons could he possibly have had?"

She looked up with a still more vivid flush. She spoke quite viciously for Nina.

"He thought I wasn't good enough for Ralph—I know he did. And, of course, I know I'm not; but Mr. Bennion needn't have told me so."

"Do you mean to say that Philip Bennion told you, in so many words, that he didn't think you were good enough for Ralph?"

"Not in so many words, but there was no mistaking what he meant. Indeed, once he said, straight out, that such

men as Ralph were not meant for girls like me. And when
I asked him what he meant, because I had done nothing
whatever to provoke the attack, he laughed—you know that
cynical little laugh he had?—and said that men like Ralph
were predestined for women of a very different class to that
which I belonged to."

"That was an odd remark for him to make."

I thought it was odder than I chose to say.   But she
departed in peace. I sent her contented away. I was not
disposed to play the part of a stony-hearted griffin, not I. I
thought that he was made for her, and that she was made
for him, that it was one of those matches which are made in
heaven. I told her so. Whereupon she kissed me and fondled
me, and made so much of me that I really began to think
that she had mistaken me for Ralph. I told her, also, that;
on which she said that I was very much in error. She would
never have dared to treat him as she was treating me—she
respected him too much; which amused me mightily.

When she had gone, leaving behind her, as it seemed
to my imagination, a pleasant savour of her presence in the
air, I fell again to examining Philip Bennion's diary.

Her words had set me wondering; recently, I had done
nothing else but wonder. I had noticed, the night before,
when looking for something else, an allusion to Nina
Macrae, which, in my cursory haste, and in the preoccu-
pation of my mind, I had failed to understand. I turned it
up again, and this time I understood it even less than I had
done before.

Here it is. It was undated, apparently entered *à propos
des bottes,* and pitchforked between memoranda of the purchase, A, of some Carolus spoons, and, B, of some Chinese
carvings.

"That jade Nina will work Ralph some mischief yet. If

he were wise he would keep away from her. I am afraid that
he has a weakness for the lures of her syren's eyes. I shall
have to give the minx a hint that she is no good for him."

What could be the meaning of such an entry as that in
Philip Bennion's diary? He wrote as if he positively disliked
the girl whom he had given all the world good reason to
believe he idolised.

To my amazement the entry was by no means an iso-
lated one. The book literally teemed with allusions to Nina.
Almost invariably they were couched in bitter and sarcastic
terms. I could not discover one in which she was referred to
kindly. The actual brutality of some of the entries was absolutely painful. They revealed Philip Bennion in a wholly unexpected phase. It was like reading his character by "flashes
of lightning," and flashes of lightning of an unpleasantly
lurid kind.

One entry in particular caught my eye. It was, to me,
so incomprehensible, that I read it over and over again, and
was still at a loss. It had been written nearly twelve months
ago.

"Jan. 11th.—N. M. has been at her tricks again. She
seems bent on keeping up her little game. Damn her! Ralph
will go stark mad if he does not take care. The girl is dangerous—there are moments when I should like to strangle
her. Has not mischief enough been done already? Heaven
knows! What are women for? The little——! Not *fiat justitia*
for me."

If I had not seen it there, in black and white, in Philip
Bennion's own penmanship, I should have judged him incapable of writing such a paragraph as that, referring to my
gentle Nina! In what spirit could it have been written? Had
I understood his complex character even less than I imagined, and had he been able to conceal from me the fact that

he had been subject to recurrent attacks of dangerous insanity?

If so, what new light might not be shed upon matters as to which I had been, and still was, wholly in the dark? If he had been, in any appreciable degree, insane—and really, when I came to think things over, I remembered how often I had thought that his eccentricities verged upon insanity—then possibly, in that fact, I might find the key to all the riddles which lately had been addling my brain.

It seemed, to me, to be inconceivable that a sane man could have treated Nina Macrae public, and even in his confidential intercourse with me, as Philip Bennion had done, and then write of her, in private, with the malevolence which disfigured the pages of his diary. What had she done to deserve it? In what had she offended him? Surely if, in any way, she had incurred his resentment or merited his reprobation, he would, at some time or the other, have dropped a hint of it, at any rate to me.

But no, not a word—not one, at any time. Never had I heard him speak of Nina Macrae—and she had been the constant theme of his conversation—except in tones of the sincerest affection, and, I might almost add, of reverential admiration.

And yet, for months and months, as far back as the diary went, he had been writing of her in terms which were not only entirely destitute of a spark of affection, but which would have only been applicable to the most abandoned of women.

To me, I say, in a sane man, the thing seemed inconceivable.

The worst of it was, that as I read and re-read the passages in Philip Bennion's diary in which Nina Macrae was alluded to, I began to wonder if it was not I who had been mistaken. If, after all, she was the sort of girl I had supposed she was.

Philip Bennion's eccentricities had only been upon the surface—superficialities, which he put off and on as he put his gloves—often designed in a spirit of mischief with a view of tormenting me. At bottom, he was as shrewd, as cool, as hard-headed, and as clear-headed a man as I ever knew. A man of catholic tastes, and with a wide knowledge of men and of things; a man who knew his world, as they have it, *aux bouts des ongles*. Never a man less likely to weigh hard upon a sinner! Witness his tolerance, even of a Mr. Raymond Clinton.

The more attentively I read those entries in his diary, the more I was compelled to ask myself if Philip Bennion had been the sort of man to write like that of any one without some cause? Whether, that is, he had been the sort of man to write, in the pages of his confidential diary, evil of a person—and that person a woman, his own ward—merely for the wanton pleasure which he felt in writing evil?

If this question had been put to me by an outsider to answer, from the knowledge which I had of the man, yes or no, I should have said, instantly and emphatically, no—never a man less likely!

It had been a marked feature of his character, as I had known him—and I should like to be told who had known him better—that he could never be induced to speak ill of a woman. There are women about of whom it is difficult to speak good—the very stones proclaim the thing!—but even of them, Philip Bennion, at any rate, would repeat no ill.

He always held that the temptations which assail women are more numerous and more irresistible than those which come to men—an opinion which is not held very strongly by the world, and for that he cried shame upon the world.

That the lines fell, for them, in harder places. That they had more of the storm and the stress and less of the joy of the fray. And when a woman went wrong, so far from saying there was no excuse for her, he insisted that there were generally millions of excuses. If all the Mary Magdalenes of the world had stood up before him in one vast array, he would have held that he, as a man, had not the smallest right to fling even the tiniest pebble at any one of them. I had always felt that, deep down in his heart, there was an inexhaustible spring of infinite, and possibly—I know not—illogical pity for the blackest sins of a woman.

Therefore, he being the man he was, it was strange to find those entries in his diary in which he alluded to Nina Macrae. The more I threshed the thing out in my mind, the less I could bring myself to believe that he would write in such a spirit—not once nor twice, but over and over again, and month after month, up to a few days before his death— without some cause, and some strong cause, too. But—angels and ministers of grace defend us!—what cause could he, of all men in the world, have had for writing evil of that flower of English maidenhood, Nina Macrae?

The entries, as I have said, extended up to a few days before he died. The last entry in which allusion was made to Nina, was dated four days before his death. It was the last entry but one the book contained—the absolutely last entry referred to a purchase of some hammered brasses which he had made the day before he died—and it was not the least curious.

It must be remembered that, at that time, Ralph Hardwicke was travelling in Italy. Philip Bennion spoke of a letter which he had received from him, and then wound up with these sufficiently remarkable words:

"Poor Ralph! I believe that minx would kill him if

she had her way—murder him, no doubt, after a fashion which would keep her out of the meshes of the avengers of blood."

What could one make of such words as those? Nina commit murder! My tender-hearted Nina; who would not hurt that proverbial nuisance, the pestiferous fly! No wonder that I closed the book with a conviction that the complication had become more complicated, that the maze was one from which there was no way out. Philip Bennion's life had been a riddle; his death had been a harder riddle; but the words which, as it were, issued from his grave presented the hardest riddle of all.

Nor did the visit which Ralph Hardwicke was destined, that night, to pay me tend much to my enlightenment; indeed, he left me with still another nut to crack.

It was not strange that I was beginning to feel, as Alice felt when she got through the looking-glass, that I had wandered into a world of cross questions and crooked answers.

CHAPTER X

WHAT RALPH HARDWICKE HAD TO SAY

ABOUT Ralph Hardwicke there was always a breezy atmosphere of health and of strength. His personality was so vigorous, that he always conveyed to all with whom he came
in contact the inevitable and instantaneous impression that,
inside and outside, the man was strong.

Nina had dropped a hint that he possibly might favour
me with a call, so that he did not take me unawares. Such
was the state of confusion into which my mental faculties
had, so to speak, meandered, that his vigorous young presence acted upon me as a pick-me-up or tonic.

He was looking well, he always did look well, but that
night I thought he was looking better than ever. His keen,
intellectual face was instinct with buoyancy and life—no
mental confusion there; but clearness of vision, directness
of purpose, force of will, and unflinching courage, which
would carry him without even a momentary hesitation by
the way, no matter what the obstacles might be which he
had to encounter, straight to the goal which he had in view.
A strong man who gloried in his strength, he made me, as,
fagged and careworn, I beheld it, glory in it too.

He came straight to the point—no sort of circumlocu-
tion for him.

"Nina has told you?"

"She has."

"And what have you to say?"

I looked at him a moment before I answered.

"Ralph, do you love her?"

"Love her!" No hesitation there. "Love her! Otway, I believe you know I am no empty boaster. There is nothing in the world which I would not do for the love of Nina."

I smiled—with the superior wisdom of cynical old age.

"You speak like a hero of romance, and, I presume, with certain mental reservations. With the man in the story, you wouldn't care to undertake to get up to make the fire for her in the mornings."

He laughed.

"I'd undertake to make the fire for her every morning of her life if she wished me to, and I'd carry out my undertaking. I'd even sacrifice my whiskers, if she wished me to do that." His cheeks and chin were as smooth as a billiard-ball, so there was safety for him there. "I'd cut my throat at a hint from her. Cut my throat! Why, Otway, I'd cut your throat—great as is my affection for you, dear old man; and every throat in Piccadilly Mansions—for the matter of that, every throat in Piccadilly—if I thought it would bring me nearer to my Nina."

I was surprised. I had not expected to hear that sort of language from him. It was a worse case even than I imagined.

He stared at me, as I sat eyeing him in silence.

"Well," he asked, repeating his first inquiry, "and what have you to say?"

"My dear Ralph, I have to thank you for the genial frankness with which you have expressed your willingness to cut my throat."

He laughed again.

"Well—and afterwards?"

"Afterwards, in wishing you joy of the best girl in the world, there is only one thing which weighs upon my mind, and that is the shade of Philip Bennion."

He started.

"Philip Bennion!"

"What is the fault he had to find with Nina?"

I watched him keenly as I put the question. He heard it with undisguised astonishment.

"What fault he had to find with Nina? Philip Bennion? Otway, what are you dreaming about?"

"Ralph, tell me frankly what was the objection he had to you and Nina becoming man and wife!"

"Objection! Not the least in the world! It was all the other way. It was understood between us that, if by dint of doing doughty deeds, if by fair means or by foul, I could win the maid, I was to win her. To see Nina my wife was the dream of his life, as well as of mine."

It was my turn to look astonished. His words suggested what I myself had always thought, and yet——

"Why did he tell Nina directly the contrary?"

"Tell Nina directly the contrary? Who? Philip Bennion?"

"Do you mean to say that you don't know that he told Nina that she was to have nothing to do with you?"

"Otway, what bee have you got in your bonnet?"

He stared as if he did not know what to make of me. I was beginning to feel that I should not know what to make of myself very soon.

"It is quite impossible that he could ever have said anything of the kind. At one time he did think I was going a little too quickly. You know, he thought that no woman ought to marry before a certain age. He might have dropped Nina a hint to that effect, but certainly nothing more."

"Suppose Nina says that he told her to have nothing to do with you, not once, but over and over again?"

"Nina must be dreaming. She is under some extraordinary delusion. Or it is possible that she mistook some of his sarcastic utterances for earnest. You know, he used to say how inapt a woman is to detect a sarcasm. It is possible that he may have been playing some of his little jokes with her. Anything else is inconceivable. Why, we arranged together, he and I, what the settlement was to be, where the marriage was to take place, where the honeymoon was to be spent, where we were to live afterwards, and even pretty well what guests were to be invited to the wedding. I am afraid"—Ralph smiled—"that we took Nina's consent for granted. Stand by a presumptuous puppy, Otway, and don't give me away. I will make my confession to the lady when—when all is safe."

He was not diminishing my sense of bewilderment. If it was as he said, what had built up such a delusion in Nina's mind? And, above all, how had those entries come to be in Philip Bennion's diary?

"Ralph," I said, conflicting doubts knocking against each other in the pandemonium which I fondly called my mind, "do you think that Philip Bennion was in any way insane?"

"Insane! Philip Bennion! Otway, what are you driving at?"

Ralph's tone of almost contemptuous surprise a little nettled me. I fancy that both my voice and my manner became a little acid.

"I have reasons of my own for asking you if you think that Philip Bennion was in any way insane."

"Reasons of your own! Really, I shall be beginning to think that you're insane."

I did not altogether like being addressed in that manner by a young man like Ralph Hardwicke.

"Suppose I have proof that he was?"

"Suppose you have—Aladdin's wonderful lamp! My

dear Otway, Philip Bennion was at all times, and in every respect, the sanest man I ever encountered—far saner than either you or I are ever likely to be."

I was silenced, but not convinced. I did not want to have a useless argument with Ralph. I thought of confronting him with those entries in the diary, but I refrained.

All at once I resolved to see if I could get any light from Ralph upon the chief point which was occupying my mind—occupying it so that it threatened to become a monomania.

"Ralph, what do you think of Philip Bennion's death?"

I had purposely asked the question without giving any sort of warning. But I was not prepared for the effect which it had on Ralph. I had momentarily forgotten how close was the attachment which had existed between the guardian and the ward.

"What do I think of—what?"

His voice distinctly trembled.

"What do you think of Philip Bennion's death?"

"Really, Otway, you appear to have prepared me a series of pleasant surprises. I think that it was the bitterest blow which has fallen upon me yet."

The young man turned away. I perceived that he felt an emotion which he did not care to let me see.

"I know that, my lad. That is not what I meant. I meant to ask you if, in the circumstances, the suddenness, the whole surroundings of Philip Bennion's death, it did not strike you that there was something—peculiar?"

"Otway, you do not appear to be yourself to-night, or else you have suddenly developed a taste for talking in riddles. Say just what you mean—right out."

I hesitated for a moment. I did not know exactly how to frame my question.

"Did it never occur to you, for a moment, to suspect that Philip Bennion might not have died of heart disease?"

Still Ralph seemed as if he were at a loss to understand me. He looked at me as if he would have liked, by the mere force of vision, to have searched out the meaning of the thoughts which were hidden in my heart. His tone became very earnest—even solemn.

"I don't know if you have forgotten, or if you think that I have forgotten, all that Philip Bennion was to me, all that I owed him. I owed to him as much as one man could owe to another. He was to me more than a father. He was to me both a companion and a friend. I do not think that he ever spoke to me one harsh or hasty word, and you know that he could, and did, speak both harsh and hasty words to other men. There was nothing, I truly believe, he had which I could not have had, and welcome. Even our thoughts we shared in common. There was no incident in my life which I withheld from him, neither great nor small. He took a greater interest in my welfare than in his own. No man ever had a more faithful friend. He was as dear to me, almost, as Nina. I fancy you have but a faint conception of what that means. Heaven alone knows what I lost when I lost him. When he went a part of me went too—something which I never shall recover. Otway, is it possible that you are suggesting that Philip Bennion met with his death by foul play?"

When he put the matter to me like that I hardly knew what to answer him.

"I do not know that I am suggesting anything. I am simply putting to you a question."

"Wasn't there an inquest held?"

"There was."

"Otway, if I thought that there was anything in any way

mysterious about the manner in which my more than father met his death, I would have the body exhumed to-morrow at my own risk and cost. For Heaven's sake, man, don't sit there like a dummy! Tell me what it is you are hinting at."

Thus pressed home, something restrained me from telling him plainly all that I was hinting at—from telling him, for instance, as plainly as I had told Mr. Raymond Clinton.

"I am a foolish old man, Ralph, and I suppose that I take fancies into my head. Philip Bennion's death was, to me, so unexpected and so sudden that I was bewildered, and I have not quite got over my bewilderment yet. A few hours before he died he was in here with me, talking about 'Murder, Considered as one of the Fine Arts.'"

Ralph regarded me with growing amazement.

"Talking about 'Murder, Considered as one of the Fine Arts?' Whatever suggested such a theme as that?"

"I don't know; one thing led to another. When he was once launched on the theme he stuck to it. He maintained that an artist in murder was one who destroyed his victim in such a manner as to leave no trace upon the body of what Bennion called his 'subject,' which would cause experts to even suspect that they were in the presence of a crime." Ralph's eyes opened wider and wider. "When in the morning we found him lying dead upon the floor of his room, I wondered if, in his case, coming events had cast their shadows before, and if he had had a premonition that he himself was about to become an example of his own theory."

"Nonsense! The thing was a coincidence, no more. So ghastly a coincidence that no wonder it worked on your imagination. Your supposititious artist in murder is an impossible person—possible in theory but not in practice. How is he going to work his wicked will? Think. Not by any sort of violence. There science would be down on him all round. A blow might leave no external mark—a blow from some sharp weapon, say the favourite needle-like stiletto of the novelist, for instance. Internal examination would make it as visible as the writing on the wall. One hears a good deal of loose talk, and one reads a good deal of inflated nonsense about insidious drugs and poisons which leave behind them no trace of their presence. The autopsy on dear old Ben was in the hands of Blakeham Warner and Lewis Cowan, two of the keenest specialists in London, and that means in the world. I wondered why you thought it necessary to call them in. Now I understand. You did quite right; otherwise, under the circumstances, there might always have been a vague doubt upon your mind, and, possibly, upon mine. No poison or drug, of any sort or kind, could conceal its presence from those two men. They might not have been able to put a name to it, but they would have seen that it was, or that it had been, there. They would have spotted that something had been present as unerringly as you would spot the nose upon my face. Science has reached a point at which, within certain limits, as a detective it is infallible. It may not be able to keep a man alive, but it is able to tell you, and that with absolute certainty, if he died from what are called natural causes. No, my dear fellow, your artist in murder is, in the present year of grace, simply and purely a creature of the imagination."

CHAPTER XI

MR. CLINTON SEES A GHOST

DURING the two or three days which followed Ralph Hardwicke's visit, I did nothing. I stagnated. I never showed my nose out of the door of my own room. I might have taken to my bed, and kept there, for all the good that I got out of life. In fact, I was seriously expecting that, in the end, I should have to take to my bed, and call in the aid of a doctor who was gifted with sufficient skill to keep my brain from turning.

I did nothing else but think—think—think. It was all very well for Ralph Hardwicke, with the confidence of youth, and health, and strength, to lay down the law, and to demonstrate, at least to his own satisfaction, that it was impossible for a man to die without the doctors being able to tell exactly what it was he died of. For my part, I doubted it. He appeared to have a higher opinion of medical science and its practitioners than I had. And, in the case of Philip Bennion, he had not had all the evidence before him.

An odd part of the matter was, that I felt an invincible repugnance to laying the evidence before him. Something held me back, kept my tongue tied, and my lips shut fast. I did not know how it was. To this hour I do not know how it was, but, for the life of me, I could not have told Ralph Hardwicke all there was to tell.

During that period of stagnation and of doing nothing else but think—think—think, I more than once had serious thoughts of calling in the assistance of the proverbial pet of Scotland Yard, or of the equally proverbial private detective. Either individual might, at any rate, be able to give me a hint. But then, on the other hand, he mightn't. I came to the conclusion that the probabilities were on the side that he mightn't. I have seen something of detectives, both public and private, in my time. There may be one in existence, somewhere, who would be of real and undoubted assistance in a difficult and delicate investigation. But not only have I never seen him, I have never even heard of him. His services are never utilised by the authorities, and his name is kept studiously out of the reported cases. I came to the conclusion that I would continue to "work the case," and, as I believe they phrase it at the "Yard," "single-handed."

A little variety was lent to the proceedings by the conduct of Mr. Raymond Clinton. He had taken to drink again. At Eton he had been troubled with thirst. It had cut short his education—at least, so far as Eton was concerned. And, as he attained to manhood, one of the more agreeable of the agreeable habits to which he was addicted was the liquor habit. Since his uncle's death I had seen nothing of his tastes in that direction. But, all at once, they came to the front again.

Several mornings, about lunch time, he came into my room, evidently suffering from a severe and well-merited headache. I could not make him out at all. He wanted to know what I had been doing. He did not seem to know whether to be angry because I had done so much, or because I had done so little. As I say, I could not make him out at all.

He also lent his mite towards the additional complication of the situation. He had an altercation with Ryan. I fancy it commenced with Ryan's refusal to allow him to knock him about when he was drunk—which Mr. Clinton considered to be impudence on the part of Ryan.

The result was that he was dismissed at a moment's notice. So all that Ryan received from Mr. Clinton, in return for his long service to Mr. Clinton's uncle, was a month's wages, no character, and the key of the street.

The morning after Ryan's dismissal Mr. Clinton came in, as usual, to me. He looked very queer—very queer indeed. After dodging about the bush a good deal, he said:

"Did you ever find out where Ryan was that night?"

"What night?"

"The night that old Ben died."

I never had found out. I had never tried to find out. I told him so.

"It's dooséd odd. Nobody seems to know. He owned himself that old Ben never gave him permission to go out. How are we to know if he ever did go out?"

I asked Mr. Clinton what he meant. He looked at me with a headachy stare, which he apparently intended should be full of meaning. "I don't know that I mean anything, exactly. But has it never occurred to you that Ryan might have known as much about how old Ben met his death as any one?"

It never had, until that moment. I wondered how many more persons would be suspected of having had a hand in Philip Bennion's premature decease.

Mr. Clinton went on:

"I never liked the way in which he gave me that link of yours, which he said that he had picked up off the floor. I always thought that he had seen you, and that he intended I should know it."

"Seen me—when?"

"That night when"—Mr. Clinton grinned—"you were walking in your sleep!"

I by no means relished the suggestion. I could have hammered Mr. Clinton's head against the wall for making it. The vista of possibilities which it opened was, from my point of view, anything but pleasant. I felt that I would have given a good round sum to know, with perfect certainty, at any rate, one thing—how many persons had figured, unconsciously to each other, in that death-chamber?

When Mr. Clinton put in his appearance on the following day he looked queerer than ever. I told myself that if he continued to look queerer, morning after morning, in that ascending ratio, he would join his uncle sooner than he either anticipated or desired.

"I say, Otway," he began, immediately on his entrance, "I'm not feeling well."

He was not looking well. He was looking very far from well. It was nearly 2 p.m., yet he seemed to have only just tumbled out of bed. His hair was unbrushed, he was apparently unwashed, and his face showed up against his gorgeous dressing-gown like badly-kneaded dough. I said nothing, but I looked at him.

"Otway," he went on, "I've seen a ghost!"

So he had already taken to "seeing things." Well, he was travelling quickly, but I was not surprised.

"You'll see more ghosts, and other things besides ghosts, if you don't practise a little moderation, Mr. Clinton."

He stared at me vacuously, with evident lack of comprehension. Then a glimpse of my meaning dawned on him.

"It wasn't that sort of thing. I know when I see that sort of thing as well as any man. And I'll take my oath I wasn't that way last night. As sure as I'm alive, Otway, I've seen a ghost!"

I eyed him. He was plainly in a state of unusual agitation, but he seemed to be sober, and, so far as I could judge, not suffering from mental derangement.

"Whose ghost have you seen?"

"By——! Otway, I've seen old Ben!"

The imprecation which he uttered to emphasise his statement fell on my ear with the force of an unpleasant jar. Almost unconsciously I assumed a sterner tone.

"Oblige me, Mr. Clinton, by not using such language in conjunction with such a theme. Where did you see this ghost of yours?"

"That's the funny part of it. By Jove! Otway, I was never in such a state before. I'm trembling now."

"That, Mr. Clinton, is certainly owing to the influence of one kind of spirit, if not of another." He eyed me angrily. The tone of his rejoinder, if characteristic, and the sort of thing which might have been expected, was scarcely civil.

"No, it's not, so don't you think it. I don't say I've not been drinking. I'm not going to deny it to any one, and certainly not to you—why should I? Suppose you listen to me, before you think yourself so clever."

I listened, and he went on; rather shakily, and with a tendency to stray from the point—but still he did go on.

"When I came home last night——"

"Was it last night or this morning?"

He looked as if he did not thank me for the interruption.

"What's that got to do with it? It was this morning, if you must have it—perhaps between three and four."

"Were you drunk?"

"I'd been drinking, but I was not drunk. It takes a lot to make me drunk."

I believed that to be the fact. I had always understood that some peculiarity in his physical constitution enabled him to swallow sufficient to stupefy two or three men without losing what he called his senses.

He stood looking at me ill-temperedly.

"Any more questions to ask?" I was perfectly placid.

"Not at present. I may have some more to ask as you go on."

He hesitated—as if he would have liked to swear—and then went on.

"As I was coming up the stairs, I had a sort of feeling as if some one was going up in front of me."

"You had a sort of feeling—how?"

"Well, I didn't see any one, and I didn't hear any one, but still I seemed to feel that there was some one there."

"I see. Or, rather, I don't see. But never mind."

"When I reached this landing I thought I saw some one dodge into the alcove—you know, that alcove in which I was that night when you went walking in your sleep."

He paused to grin. He was always dragging in, on all possible occasions, so to speak, by the head and shoulders, an allusion to that little episode; which custom of his lent, so far as I was concerned, a constant flavour to his conversation—more especially as, on each occasion, he invariably paused to emphasise the allusion with a grin.

Just then I allowed his little display of genial humour to go apparently unnoticed. So he went on:

"When I came to the last step or two I could have bet a hat that some one on the landing turned round, saw me coming, and dodged into the alcove."

"Wasn't there a light?"

"There never is much of a light at that hour of the morning. The beggar of a porter pretends there is, but there's just about enough to let you see a haystack just as you are running into it."

My experience was otherwise. As a matter of fact, the staircases are lighted throughout the night by electricity.

But as I thought it extremely probable that circumstances over which he *had* control had dimmed Mr. Clinton's vision, I made no comment.

"I stopped on the landing, and I said, 'Come out of that!' No one came, so I went to the alcove to rout the beggar out, whoever he might be. It gave me quite a turn when I found there was no one there. I could have sworn I saw some one dodge into it! 'This is dooséd funny,' I said; 'I wonder if old Otway's walking in his sleep again.'"

Another allusion—dragged in by the head and ears—and, of course, the accompanying grin.

"I listened, but I heard nothing, and there was nothing to be seen. So I turned into my rooms. I went straight to my bedroom, and began to undress. But all the time I felt quite certain that some one was in the drawing-room. I don't know what made me feel like that, because I could hear nothing, and, of course, with my door closed I couldn't see; but I'll take my oath that I did feel certain. At last, just as I was going to turn in between the sheets, I couldn't stand it any longer—I was all upon the fidget. 'Hang it,' I said, 'if I don't see who's there.' So I opened my bedroom door, and went across the dressing-room and opened the drawing-room door. Otway, there was some one there—by——! there was."

Mr. Clinton paused, perceptibly shuddered, and looked about him with wild, uncertain eyes. I could see that it required an effort on his part to enable him to go on.

"It was quite light. You know, I haven't had a fellow since that beastly Ryan hooked it, and I had forgotten to turn off the electric light. In fact, I hardly ever do when I come in; I leave it burning till the morning, it's such an awful bore."

Touching an ivory button was such an awful bore!

"I could see everything in the place as plainly as I can see you now. And I could see that some one was standing at old Ben's writing-table. He was stooping down, and he had his back towards me, so at first I could not see who it was. But I went funny directly I saw that there was some one there. How the deuce had he got in? But I went funnier a moment afterwards, when I saw—by——! it was old Ben! I suppose I must have made a noise or something, because all at once he stood up, and I saw it was old Ben."

Mr. Clinton paused to wipe his brow. From the state of agitation he was in one could see that, at any rate, the vision had seemed real enough to him.

As he seemed incapable of going on without assistance, I helped him with a question.

"What did you do then?"

He made an evident attempt to regain his self-control.

"I suppose I must have fallen down in a fit or something, because when I came to I found myself lying all in a heap on the ground. I tell you I didn't stop to see if old Ben was still inside, but I made straight off to bed as fast as my legs would carry me. And there I've stuck until just now. And then I felt that I must come out and tell you what I'd seen, although I knew you'd laugh at me."

I did not laugh at him. I wondered.

"How do you know it was your uncle?"

"How do I know? Do you think that I shouldn't know old Ben among a million, let alone when I saw him within a dozen yards of me?"

"Did you see his face?"

"I didn't get as far as that. I knew him directly he moved, then I suppose that I went off at once."

"You must excuse my remarking, Mr. Clinton, that you don't appear, on this occasion, to have been conspicuous for presence of mind."

He looked rueful, even in the midst of his agitation.

"No, I know I don't; and that's what riles me. But the sight of old Ben, looking for all the world as if he were alive and kicking, took me so aback. I hadn't been thinking of him in the least."

"You say that all the time you were undressing you felt quite certain that some one was in the drawing-room. Who did you think was there?"

"I had not the faintest notion. I only felt that there was some one there."

"How was this person, whom you suppose to have been your uncle, dressed?"

Mr. Clinton hesitated.

"I didn't notice. I have a sort of general impression that he was dressed in black, but all that I'm certain about is that it was old Ben."

I gave expression to an idea which had occurred to me.

"How do you know that it wasn't Ryan?"

"Ryan!" Mr. Clinton stared. "Do you think that I shouldn't know Ryan? Besides, what on earth should he be doing there?"

"That I cannot tell you. But granting that you saw some one, which has yet to be proved, it seems, to put it mildly, more likely to have been Ryan than your uncle."

My suggestion that proof was required of his having seen any one seemed to annoy him.

"There isn't much proof wanted about that, because, as I came to you, I came through the drawing-room, just to see if old Ben was still there; and the first thing I saw was that a drawer was open in the writing-table over which I had seen him stooping."

"You say that the drawer was open when you came in here?"

"Wide open—pulled right out."

"Didn't you open it yourself?"

"Open it myself! I haven't touched that writing-table since the night that you were there; and, by the way, it's the very drawer out of which I took old Ben's diary which I gave you."

His words struck me.

"Is that drawer still open?"

"I suppose it is, unless it's shut itself of its own accord since I came in here?"

"Can I look at it?"

"If you like you can. Look here, Otway, who do you think you're getting at? If you think that I'm playing it off on you, or that I've had a touch of D. T., or anything of that sort, you're wrong. I saw old Ben last night as sure as I see you now—I'll stake my life on it."

"I am not contradicting you. Let us go and look at this drawer."

We went and looked at the drawer. When we entered that now historic drawing-room, which Philip Bennion loved in life, and which, according to his nephew, he bade fair to haunt in death, I looked round to see if there were about the place any signs of obvious disorder. Nothing of the kind, however, was noticeable—nothing, that is, which might not be expected in an apartment which was occupied by Raymond Clinton.

"Have you missed anything?" I asked.

"Missed anything? What do you mean? Do you think that I mistook burglars for old Ben?"

"If you saw any one at all, I think it is extremely probable that it was some one who came here to look for something he particularly wanted. Whether it was money or not, I cannot say. He was interrupted by your appearance, and that that is so the evidence of the open drawer, which he had not time to close, is, to my mind, sufficient proof."

For the drawer was still open—the identical drawer, as Mr. Clinton had said, from which he had taken Philip Bennion's diary. The contents had apparently been tampered with. They were all tumbled about. But, as Mr. Clinton himself remarked, he was a "deuce of a hand at messing up a drawer," it was possible that the interior had been found in a state of disorder when the drawer was opened.

"I suppose," I said, "that you don't know all that was in it?"

"Not I. All I know is that there were a lot of papers and things—principally receipted bills, I fancy, for the things in old Ben's collection."

If that were so, then they were gone. I emptied the contents of the drawer out upon the writing-table.

"There are no bills here now."

"No. That's dooséd odd. Look again. I'll swear that the drawer was half-full of them."

I did look again. We both of us looked. We looked everywhere, turning out the other drawers as well. There was not a trace of anything of the kind to be seen.

"It strikes me, Mr. Clinton, that if you had drunk a little less, or kept your presence of mind a little more, you would have seen very good cause for handing over your uncle's 'ghost' to the tender custody of the police."

When he perceived that there was not so much as a vestige of a bill remaining, he seemed himself to realise that there might be something in what I said.

"But what on earth could Ryan, or any one, want with a lot of old, paid bills?"

"Ah—what?"

I wondered, without imparting my wonder to Mr. Clinton, if Ryan, or any one, would have liked to have had Philip Bennion's diary as well.

CHAPTER XII

THE TOXICOLOGIST'S REPORT

"MY DEAR SIR,

"I propose to call on you to-morrow morning at half-past ten with reference to the key which you requested me to examine and report upon.

"If the hour or date is not convenient, I should be obliged by your letting me have a line to that effect.

"But the key is such a peculiar key, that, instead of merely handing you a written report, I should like to see you, if possible, in person.

"Yours obediently,
"LEWIS COWAN.

"J. Franklyn Otway, Esq."

This was the note which lay in front of me, as I awaited Mr. Cowan's arrival. Possibly, when he had had his say, matters might be advanced one step further out of the *cul-de-sac* which, it seemed to me, they had entered.

It was a few minutes after the appointed time when Mr. Cowan appeared. He was a little, active, wiry-looking man, with that sphinx-like expression of features which is seen in a certain type of Jew.

I rose as he came in.

"Come, Mr. Cowan, we will talk while we are having breakfast."

"Breakfast!" He did not look amazed, because his is the sort of face which could never look amazed. But his voice betrayed amazement. "My good sir, I breakfast every morning of my life at seven. No breakfast for me."

Which was hard upon me, because I did not breakfast at seven, and I wanted to breakfast then. Indeed, I had been waiting for his arrival to begin. But before I could suggest that he would at least allow me to feed, he wheeled round, in the quick way he had, and saw the Medici cabinet. I had had it brought over from Mr. Clinton's apartments only the day before—desirous of making sure of my three thousand guineas' worth—and a very good appearance in my room it made.

"Ah!" exclaimed Mr. Cowan, who seemed to arrive at his conclusions by some process of intuition. "That is the cabinet to which the key belongs. I see." He went across the room to it. "It is a good cabinet." Pause. "It is a very good cabinet." Another pause. "It is the finest cabinet I ever saw. That cabinet and key have a history, Mr. Otway. May I ask you where you got them from?"

"They were the property of my friend, the late Philip Bennion."

"And may I ask where he got them from?"

"He purchased them, I believe, from a dealer in the Brompton Road."

"From a dealer in the Brompton Road? I imagine that there are few dealers in the Brompton Road, or elsewhere, who have cabinets like that to sell. When I last saw that cabinet it was in Rome."

"You have seen it before?"

Mr. Cowan's incisive manner and rapid utterance a little took my breath away. Then my appetite was keen—it generally is in the morning—and I knew that breakfast was on the table in the next room, and that it was probably spoiling. Altogether I felt a trifle flurried.

"I have. I saw it when it was in Rome. It was in the Fiezza Palace."

"In the Fiezza Palace?"

The cabinet was becoming more mysterious still. It was through the irony of fate that it had fallen to my lot to unravel all these tangled threads; no man ever less liked mysteries. How came it to travel from the Fiezza Palace to the Brompton Road? A similar reflection seemed to have occurred to Mr. Cowan.

"It was in one of the private rooms. When I saw that key I wondered if it could belong to that cabinet. I thought that there could scarcely be two such keys and two such cabinets. I don't know if you are aware that the story goes that that cabinet belonged to Lucrezia Borgia. They say that that is her portrait in the two upper panels. But they say all sorts of things. Have you any notion what your friend gave to that dealer in the Brompton Road?"

"I have reason to believe that he gave a hundred guineas."

"A hundred guineas!" Mr. Cowan whistled. "If this gentleman had not been your friend, Mr. Otway, I should say that this had been a case of a receiver and a thief."

I said nothing. It was a painful admission to have to make, even to oneself, but I felt that it was quite possible that Philip Bennion would not have been deterred from driving a bargain, with a view to enriching his collection, even if he had felt confident that the object he desired had been obtained under circumstances which, to say the least of it, were shady. Those collectors are marvellous beings. I have known men who, as ordinary individuals, have been the soul of honesty, as collectors do the most amazing things. I have heard of collectors—men of the highest standing—stealing coveted specimens from other collectors, and that without a twinge of conscience or the suspicion of a blush.

Perceiving that I continued silent, Mr. Cowan wheeled round to me.

"However, that is not the point. Here is the key which you asked me to examine." He produced it from a box which he took out of his overcoat pocket. "Is the cabinet locked?" I told him it was. "I don't know if you are aware that to unlock it the key has to be turned in the reverse direction. If you attempt to turn it in the usual direction it means mischief. Thus!"

Inserting the key in the lock he turned it, instead of from left to right, from right to left. It turned quite easily. The door came open.

"If you wish to lock the cabinet you don't use the key, but you press the door to with your hand, and it locks with a spring. Thus!"

Again he gave his words practical illustration.

"The key comes to pieces. See, I will unscrew it. It is made in three distinct parts—handle, barrel, wards."

As he spoke he did unscrew it. As he said, each part was, so to speak, complete in itself. He held the three parts, separated, in his hand.

"In the barrel there is a most ingenious mechanical contrivance. It consists, first of all, of a small but powerful spring. It is released by the handle, when it is attached to the barrel, being turned from left to right, as you would turn an ordinary key in opening an ordinary lock. On being released, this spring projects upwards a small stiletto—projects it upwards with very considerable force. This stiletto is hollow throughout its entire length, and open at the point—like, for instance, a stylographic pen. At the extremity it has a movable cap—again like some varieties of the stylographic pen. The spring not only projects the stiletto upwards, but, after it has attained a certain elevation, it presses against the cap. If, therefore, the stiletto—which, you will remember, is hollow—is filled with liquid matter, the pressure upon the cap drives a few drops of this liquid through the opening at the point. You understand?"

I did understand. I understood only too well.

"An ingenious contrivance, is it not?"

"You call it ingenious! I call it a diabolical contrivance."

"The language one uses depends upon one's point of view. I call it an ingenious contrivance. When the key reached me the stiletto contained liquid matter. It was not full; it was perhaps nearly three-parts full."

"What was the nature of the stuff which it contained?"

"It was of a poisonous nature. I proved that by actual experiment. A single minute injection almost killed a cat, and it quite killed a kitten—and that in an instant. But it had a peculiar property. It was on the Tuesday that it had the effect which I have mentioned upon the cat and kitten. But on the Thursday immediately following it had no perceptible effect whatever upon a cat, and only a temporary effect upon a kitten. It was evident, therefore, that its poisonous nature was evanescent. I have no doubt that when the stiletto was originally filled, it was both more rapid and more deadly in its action. Not the least peculiar fact of the matter, from my point, is that the poison, as a poison, is entirely strange to me. It appears to be vegetable, and I should conjecture that it came from India. But beyond that I am entirely at sea. Can you tell me anything about it, Mr. Otway?"

"I can tell you nothing. I looked to you to tell me everything. My friend, Philip Bennion, bought the cabinet from a dealer who, at that time, had a shop in the Brompton Road, and who called himself Richard Gent. The key did not come home with the cabinet, but it arrived two or three days afterwards. My friend mislaid it on the night of its arrival. It was not found till after his death, which occurred some six months afterwards. I then found it, quite by accident, and I handed it there and then to Mr. Clinton, who is my friend's nephew and his heir. It was only when Mr. Clinton, on putting it in the lock and turning it, was struck senseless and almost killed, that we discovered that there was anything peculiar in its construction. And on the following morning I forwarded it you for your examination and report."

"And you mean to say that your friend, the purchaser, had no notion that there was anything unusual either about the cabinet or its key?"

"I cannot say positively, but I believe not. He was my most intimate friend. He showed me the cabinet on the day that it came from the dealer's, and he hinted at nothing of the kind. As I tell you, the key did not come with the cabinet. He mentioned, quite casually, that it wanted cleaning or something, he did not quite know what, and that it was to follow."

"And, when it did come, he did not use it?"

"No. It came home just as he was starting for dinner. He put it down in a hurry. In the morning, when he looked for it, he could not remember where."

"And it was not found till after his death?"

"So far as I know."

I hesitated. Mr. Cowan was silent. I perceived that he saw that I had something to add. So I broached the matter which had, all the time, been weighing on my mind.

"The friend I am alluding to was Mr. Philip Bennion. You, possibly, remember the circumstances of his death?"

"Were not the contents of his stomach submitted to me for my analysis?"

"They were. And, as you will remember, you stated what was the result of your analysis in the evidence which you gave at the inquest."

"I remember."

"Mr. Cowan, when I handed you that key, what I wished chiefly to learn from you was if you thought it possible that it had anything to do with Philip Bennion's death."

His answer was prompt, emphatic, and to the point.

"Not the slightest."

I had expected some such answer as that; but I had not expected quite such a demonstration of assured conviction.

"Excuse me, Mr. Cowan, but may I presume that you are sure of that?"

"Quite sure."

"Pardon me still further, but may I ask you to give me some idea of what are the grounds of your assurance?"

"I am not able to tell you exactly what the poison which was in the barrel of that key is, but I should be able to detect its presence in the body of a person who had been killed by it. Examination even by an ordinary practitioner would reveal it. Its method of action, although curious, is unmistakable. It produces a sort of paralysis, something analogous to that which is seen in a case of tetanus. This appearance—of acute paralytic contraction of the muscles—continues to be visible long after death. Judging from the body of the kitten, I should say that this appearance is immovable. In the case of Philip Bennion nothing of the kind was seen. The condition of the body was entirely normal."

Then he added something for which I was unprepared.

"Frankly, when you sent me that key, being aware of your intimacy with Mr. Bennion, I suspected what might be passing through your mind. So, before I came to you, I consulted with Dr. Blakeham Warner, who, you recollect, also gave evidence. He agrees with me that Mr. Bennion could not possibly have come into active contact with the contents of that key."

In my anxiety to relieve myself of some of the bewildering doubts which beset me, I asked what was doubtless an unreasonable question.

"But who could have put that poison in the key, and what was the purpose which it was designed to fulfil?"

"That I cannot tell you." He fixed his inscrutable glance upon my countenance. "What cause have you to suspect that Mr. Bennion met with his death otherwise than in the ordinary course of nature?"

"Mr. Cowan, I do not know if I have or have not cause. But I will tell you."

Then I told him what the reader knows already. He listened attentively, never removing his eyes from off me. When I had finished he made an almost exactly similar remark to that which Ralph Hardwicke had made.

"That conversation on murder which you had with your friend the night before he died was a coincidence."

"I have asked myself over and over again if it was only a coincidence."

"Why should it have been more?" He paused. He looked at me as a cat might look at a mouse. "Mr. Otway, whom do you suspect?"

I hesitated. Should I tell him about my dream, and of my suspicions of Raymond Clinton? I decided that I would not. So I hedged:

"I do not know that I can be said to have actually suspected any one. Vague doubts have crossed my mind from time to time. Mr. Cowan, I look to you to resolve these doubts. Candidly, can you tell me, between man and man, that you are absolutely certain that Philip Bennion owed his death to natural causes?"

Mr. Cowan seemed to reflect. A sardonic smile played about his lips.

"I will tell you this much, Mr. Otway, that I can tell you nothing. Laymen appear to have curious ideas of the present state of medical science. Your friend's artist in murder is a perfectly practicable personage. It is possible to commit murder in a thousand different ways without leaving behind the slightest trace of a crime. If that cabinet and key were sold to Mr. Bennion with intent to murder—and one cannot but perceive that there were circumstances which point that way—then I can only remark that it at least is possible that the person who had that intention, finding himself foiled in one direction, was capable of a new and even more skilfully artistic development of his homicidal tendencies. You heard my statement at the inquest. I spoke to the evidence. If the same evidence is before me, I am prepared to repeat that statement tomorrow. If, on the other hand, you have fresh evidence in my line to lay before me, I am prepared to give it my careful consideration."

As Mr. Cowan continued to speak, my heart seemed gradually to cease beating. I knew that I was trembling.

"Then you do believe that Philip Bennion was murdered!"

He smiled again.

"I believe nothing. I do not deal in beliefs. I say that if you have, either now or at any other time, fresh evidence in my line to lay before me, I am, and shall be, prepared to give it my careful consideration. And I say further, that your late friend, Mr. Bennion's theoretical artist in murder is a perfectly practicable personage."

CHAPTER XIII

FACE TO FACE WITH THE MEDICI CABINET

My suspicions had been waxing and waning. Originally, when I had come upon my friend lying dead, I had been completely persuaded, as if inspired by a revelation from on high, that he had come to his death by the act of man. I could have cried aloud to the world, such was the strength of my innate conviction, that Raymond Clinton had slain his uncle. But, as day followed day, and I listened to the medical evidence, I came to look at the matter with calmer eyes. I could not but feel that, in this respect, I might have been doing Mr. Clinton an injustice. After our discovery of the key of the cabinet, and after he had told me his story of what he did on that eventful night, almost unconsciously to myself, my suspicions of his blood-guiltiness faded into nothing.

When circumstances pointed to the impossibility of Philip Bennion's having used that key, and I failed to light upon any other sort of clue, and could not conceive who, in the whole wide world, would wish to work him ill, I began by degrees to believe that, after all, the doctors might have been in the right and I in the wrong, and that the dead man might have come to his death by the sudden operation of one of the ordinary laws which govern our physical constitution.

But, after Mr. Cowan had gone, there came back to me a sickening certainty that my original suspicions had been justified, and that Philip Bennion had not met with his death in the ordinary course of nature. It was not so much what Mr. Cowan had said—he was far too cautious to commit himself in actual words—as the manner in which he had said it, which made it clear to my mind, that he himself thought that it, at least, was extremely probable, that the verdict returned by the coroner's jury had not declared the truth.

I felt that he believed, what I myself had believed from the first, that we might be, and probably were, in the presence of that creation of the dead man's brain—the ideal Artist in Murder.

My appetite had pretty nearly vanished, and it was with a feeling of depression weighing heavily upon me that I sat down to the overcooked mockery of my morning's meal. I knew that I should suffer from indigestion, as I swallowed a few mouthfuls of the dishes which had been cooked out of all semblance of their proper form. The knowledge that I should so suffer did not tend to raise my spirits, and it was with a pessimistic consciousness that for me life was rapidly becoming not worth living that I returned into my sitting-room.

Mr. Cowan had left the key in a little open box upon the table. The parts were still divided. I sat looking at the box, and the key, and the cabinet with a morbid feeling settling upon my brain that, after all, it would perhaps be quite as well if I had gone one step further in that sleep-walking experience of mine, and if I really had destroyed my friend. It seemed to me, in the mood in which I then was, that I might as well hang—even for such a crime as that—as continue to live the life which I had been living.

I was still wrapped in such-like dark imaginings when I was interrupted by the entrance of Ralph Hardwicke and his affianced wife, Nina Macrae. I do not know that I was glad to see them. I do not think I was. There was about them, as it seemed to me just then, too aggressive an air of youth, and health, and hope, and happiness. Upon their sky there seemed to be no possibility of cloud. I was half conscious of a sort of resentment that this should be so.

Ralph came and shook my hand, using his young giant's strength just like a giant, until I thought he would have crushed it into a shapeless mass. I was not obliged to him for that. And Nina knelt beside me, and put her arms about my neck, and kissed me, and insisted on a recognition of her caresses which I was ill-disposed to give her.

"Guardian," she began, "you and I shall quarrel. When I came to you before you were not looking well. Now you are looking worse than ever. What have you got upon your mind?"

"Suicide," I said.

"Suicide!" she cried.

"Yes, suicide," I snarled. It was a snarl—for she and Ralph were positively smiling. "Suicide is what I said, and suicide is what I meant."

"I see what will have to happen," she observed. "You will have to be taken in hand by a sensible person—like me—and then we'll see if suicide is what you mean." She turned to her lover. "Ralph, tell this wicked person what it is we've come about. Perhaps that will raise his thoughts to the contemplation of higher things."

Ralph laughed.

"I doubt it," he declared.

"You doubt it! How dare you, sir! Ralph, tell him the news at once."

Ralph disposed himself to take his ease upon the couch.

"You! You will tell it so much better than I—you have that delicacy which I most lack."

"Are you ashamed, sir, of what we have come to tell?"

"No—that is, not in any appreciable degree—more than does become a man."

She turned to me, her eyes all flashing, her face alive with mock anger, and with laughter, and with love.

"You hear him! Should I tell you of what he is not ashamed in any appreciable degree, more than does become a man? We have fixed the day. That is what we have come to tell you, and that is what he is not ashamed of—in any appreciable degree."

"You have fixed the day for what? For suicide?"

"Guardian!" She shrank away from me. "How can you! It is our wedding-day that we have fixed."

"I have read in some old book that the words are synonymous—marriage and suicide."

Ralph, lying on the couch, laughed out.

She, pretending to be hurt by my words, stood up.

"Guardian! Can anything equal the wickedness of men!" She sighed. "Yet, after all, I suppose that you are right, and that it is a sort of suicide—for the woman that is wed."

She had me there, and knew she had me. And she looked so sweet, and, not to put too fine a point on it, so kissable, that she almost charmed the sullen mood right out of me.

"If," I said, with a final resolve to preserve some fragment of my grimness, "to the woman it is suicide, then, to a certainty, it's murder to the man."

Hardly had the words escaped my lips, than in her bearing I noticed a curious change.

I sat at the table. Ralph lay at my left, upon the couch. She stood at my right. When she had first entered the room she had made straight for me, and without noticing anything else, had instantly prisoned me with her two arms.

It seemed, therefore, that it was only when, in her prettily simulated anger, she had shrunk away from me, and stood upon her feet, that she noticed that my room had received an addition to the ornaments which it contained, and that that addition took the shape of the Medici cabinet.

I could not make out, for a moment, what it was that was causing her to fix such an intensity of gaze upon the opposite side of the room. Then I perceived that she was looking at my three thousand guineas' worth of cabinet.

Still I could not understand what could possibly be causing her to regard it in so singular a manner. She was staring at it with parted lips and widely dilated eyes, as if she were staring at a ghost.

Ralph and I were both observing her with wonder.

"Hallo, Nina, what's the matter?" cried Ralph, half laughingly.

She paid no attention to his question. But she said, speaking, as it seemed to me, with a degree of tragic intensity which such an inquiry scarcely justified:

"Where did you get that from?"

I was puzzled. Her emotion was so sudden, so uncalled-for; the change from jest to earnest so almost unnaturally complete.

"Where did I get what from? The cabinet?"

"The poisoned cabinet."

The words were gasped rather than spoken. I was startled.

"Nina!" I exclaimed.

Rising from the couch, Ralph advanced to soothe her. It really seemed that she required soothing.

"What is the matter with you, child?" he asked.

She turned to him a face which had become all at once transformed. She grasped his arms with her two hands. She looked at him with eyes which positively blazed. She spoke to him in a voice the like of which I had never heard from Nina.

"Ralph, where did he get it from? I saw that cabinet in Rome—they said it belonged to Lucrezia Borgia—it is the poisoned cabinet!"

Ralph spoke to her almost as if he had been speaking to a baby.

"My dear child, what are you talking about?"

But I was more amazed than I could say. She had unconsciously endorsed Mr. Cowan's statement as to the cabinet's original home.

"You saw it in Rome?" I cried.

She turned on me like some wild thing.

"Yes—in Rome! How did it come here?"

"It belonged to Philip Bennion."

"Oh, my God!"

She sank on her knees beside the table; she covered her face with her hands; she trembled as an aspen trembles which is shaken by the wind. I was astonished out of the power of speech. What was the meaning of it all?

Ralph, after what seemed to be a glance of inquiry at me, endeavoured to assuage her agitation. Falling on one knee beside her, he put his arm about her waist.

"Nina, what magic spell has suddenly bewitched you? What is the latest fancy which, all at once, has stolen into your fanciful head, you mistress of all strange fancies!"

Taking her hands from before her face she looked at him with wild, eager, searching eyes. She spoke with a little break in her voice.

"Ralph, you—you will always love me? Won't you, Ralph?"

Ralph's voice, as he answered her, was soft, and deep,

and full of music—full of that music which, they tell us, is the sweetest of all music to a woman's ear.

"Always, sweetheart—for ever and for aye!"

Throwing her arms about his neck, she kissed him with what almost seemed to be an hysterical outburst of affection.

"My darling—oh, my darling!"

Ralph laughingly reminded her of my presence.

"Sweetheart, are you forgetting that we are not alone?"

"It's only guardian," she said. And, as she said it, she looked up at me with some fragmentary return of the mischief of her smile. "Guardian doesn't count."

She stood up, disengaging as she did so Ralph's arm from about her waist. But in her manner there still was something which was strange to me. The thing was made more obvious by the effort which she made to pass it off as nothing.

"Of course I remember that cabinet, I remember it very well. I noticed it when guardian"—she checked herself with a sort of little gasp—"I mean, when Mr. Bennion brought it home. He showed it me. And, of course, I saw it many times after that. I remember just where it stood in his room." She paused; then she added, looking at me with a gratuitous defiance in her eyes and in her bearing, which made me wonder more and more what there was in me she need defy: "And I couldn't make up my mind, but each time I saw it I was always thinking that I had seen it somewhere before—I mean, before I saw it in Mr. Bennion's room. Now it all comes back to me quite clearly. It is the cabinet which I saw in the Fiezza Palace at Rome, and which they said belonged to Lucrezia Borgia. I am sure of it—oh yes, I am quite sure."

The defiant ring in her voice, and the defiant gaze in her eyes, as she reiterated her assurance, brought to me a new revelation of Nina Macrae.

Ralph Hardwicke had also risen to his feet, and while his lady-love was favouring me with unexpected recollections of the tragic stage, he had sauntered over to the cabinet. He now stood regarding it with the appreciative admiration of a capable and a sympathetic critic.

"A fine thing. As an example, I should say, almost unique. I also remember it, in the dear old fellow's room, though not at Rome." He spoke with a touch of dryness, which, unless I am mistaken, made Nina start. "Otway, how came it here?"

Nina echoed his inquiry. But with this difference, that while his tone betrayed carelessness, hers betrayed unmistakable defiance. Defiance of what, I was more and more at a loss to understand.

"Yes, that is just what I was about to ask—how came it here?"

I replied, almost with an air of deprecation, feeling as if I had been guilty of some crime:

"Mr. Clinton gave it to me. He thought that I would like a memento of my friend. He asked me what I would like to choose, so I chose that."

"Oh!" Nina drew a long breath. She never removed, for an instant, her eyes from off my face, nor softened in one tittle the hard defiance of her stare. "You chose that. I see."

Ralph's laughing voice came from the cabinet.

"And not a bad choice either, for a man who does not profess to much knowledge of such things. I do not think that you could have chosen anything much better worth the having, eh, Nina?"

"No, I don't think he could." She turned towards him

with the stiffness of an automaton. Then, in the utterance of an exclamation, all her stiffness vanished. "What's this?" she cried.

Her glance had fallen on the little open box which contained the separated parts of what Mr. Cowan had called that "ingenious contrivance" in the way of keys. She stooped over it, repeating in a sort of frenzy her own words.

"What's this—what's this? It's the key! It's unscrewed!" She actually clenched her fists as she stood up and faced me. "What's the meaning of this?" she cried.

As I stood staring at her, momentarily dumb in my amazement, Ralph approached her from behind. It was he who spoke:

"Nina, are you quite sure that you're quite well? What's the meaning of what, young woman?" He perceived the little box. "What's this? A key?" He took it up into his hand. "The key of the cabinet? Is this what causes my dearest lady such concern? Sweetheart, where's the wonder? Why, it's in pieces. Hallo, Otway, what have you been doing?"

"Yes," cried Nina, her aggressive tones in curious contrast to her lover's tones of placid curiosity, "what have you been doing?"

I passed my hand across my brow. I felt that I really should go mad if something did not happen soon which would supply me with a plausible answer to all these riddles.

"There was something about the key which I could not altogether understand, so I submitted it to Lewis Cowan for his examination."

Ralph looked at me with wondering eyes.

"Do you mean that you submitted it to Cowan, the man who is great on poisons?"

"I do."

"What did you do that for?"

"More out of curiosity, I fancy, than anything else."

Ralph looked at me as if he could not make me out, which was not strange. I could not make myself out just then. I should have been very sorry to have been compelled to furnish that minute analysis of my emotions of which, in fiction, the present generation appears to be so fond.

Nina's conduct was amazing. She came and grasped my arm with a vigour and a strength which I found to be not a little disconcerting.

"What did he say?" she gasped.

"What did who say? My dear, you hurt my arm."

"Mr. Cowan—quick, what did he say?"

As she increased rather than decreased her pressure on my arm, I deemed it expedient to reply to her question with such haste as I had at my command.

"He said—my dear, you are really hurting me—he said—good gracious!—he said that the key was charged with poison."

She said nothing. She released my arm in a manner which was almost as disconcerting as was the actual ferocity with which she had grasped me. With some distant resemblance to the movements of a pendulum, she wavered for a moment in the air. Then she did a thing of which I had never thought that Nina Macrae could have been capable: she fell to the ground in a dead faint—just as they do that sort of thing upon the stage. I was thunderstruck.

I don't know what was on Ralph Hardwicke's face as we both of us stood looking down at her. But I know that on mine there was something which I would have given all that I possessed to have kept from it.

CHAPTER XIV

I TAKE A WALK

IT was on the morning of the day previous to that on which Ralph and Nina were to be married that I took a walk, every incident of which, if the tales which the scientists tell us are true, will be found vividly impressed upon the retina of my brain, if I live to twice the allotted span of man. It was not so much the incidents themselves which were impressive, as the catastrophe was overwhelming which they immediately led up to.

That evening Ralph was to fetch me to have dinner with him at his club. He was to call for me on his way. That dinner was to serve as a sort of farewell to his bachelor life. He and I, as it were, were to see out together his life of "single cursedness"—see it out together in a civil and unostentatious way. On the morrow he was to embark on that unknown sea—unknown so far as I am concerned—which men call matrimony. For him there would be no more bachelor dinners at the club. So, as was fitting, at that last dinner, which almost attained the dignity of a "function," the old and the young bachelor were to dine together.

I had not sauntered far along the pavement in the direction of Piccadilly Circus, when I met, to use a figure of speech, with the first puff of wind which was to ruffle the surface of the unwonted peace which filled my mind.

The puff of wind took the shape—the non-figurative shape—of Ryan.

I had not seen him since, in a fit of temper, Mr. Clinton had dismissed him from his service, and when I again did see him I was not favourably impressed by the change which

had taken place in his appearance. I never had been, as I perhaps need scarcely observe, in Mr. Ryan's confidence, but it
was only reasonable to suppose that during his many years'
service under so liberal a master as Philip Bennion, he would
have availed himself of at least some of the opportunities
which offered, to lay by something for a rainy day. It came
upon me, therefore, with a sort of shock, when I observed
in his personal appearance the unmistakable signs of being
hard up.

He saw me first, and came across the road to speak to
me.

"Well, Ryan," I said, "how goes the world with you?"

"Very bad, sir. About as bad as it very well can do."

"I'm sorry to hear that."

I was sorry. It seemed to me that I had known Ryan almost as long as I had known Philip Bennion. Indifferent servant though he was—and Bennion had forgiven him both
much and often—he was the first and last servant my friend
had ever had.

"Are you still out of a situation? Or have you given up
service altogether?"

"I think, sir, that service has given me up altogether. It
seems that it's against a man to remain in one service his
whole life long. Gentlemen don't want old servants, they
want young ones."

I was conscious that there was something in what he
said. He was as old as I was. His age might not be in his
favour.

"Is there anything I can do for you?"

"Well, sir, if you could give me a character; you know almost as much about me as Mr. Bennion did. Mr. Clinton"—
Ryan's face grew dark—"says he'll see me d——d before he
says a word for me, and Miss Macrae's not much good as a

reference. Gentlemen don't want a valet's character from a young lady."

"Miss Macrae! Has she offered you a reference?"

"Yes, sir, she has. She saw me the other day, and she stopped me. She asked me a lot of questions about a lot of things—principally about a cabinet the governor had——"

I interrupted him.

"A cabinet? What cabinet!"

"I dare say you remember it, sir. An Italian cabinet it was. The governor bought it about six months before he died. He made a great fuss because he lost the key. It came home one night, and he put it somewhere, and then he couldn't find it in the morning; he couldn't think where he'd put it. Miss Macrae wanted to know if he ever found it before he died. She seemed to think that he did. I don't know what made her think so. I don't think he ever did, and so I told her."

I was conscious that the pulsations of my heart all at once had quickened. Was that ancient piece of furniture destined always to intrude?

"I am rather interested in that cabinet myself, Ryan; I know the one which you refer to. Did Miss Macrae tell you what made her think that Mr. Bennion found the key?"

"No, sir, she didn't. But if I may make so bold as to say so, she didn't seem to be quite herself. When I said that I didn't think he did, she went quite funny. I thought she was going to faint. She clenched her fists and looked up at the sky, and said, in a tone of voice which, out in the street there, and before all the people, made me feel quite shivery like, 'But I know he did!' I don't know what makes her know, because, as I say again, I don't believe he ever did."

When I left Ryan, which I did after assisting him to the extent of a couple of sovereigns, and telling him that he might refer any one to me who wanted to know his antecedents, I left him with the consciousness of that "little rift in the lute, which makes all the music mute."

Nor did another incident, which occurred almost immediately after I had quitted Ryan, tend to increase my cheerfulness.

As I neared the Circus I became aware that a woman was walking, or rather staggering, at my side, and endeavouring to address me. I first became aware of it by the fact of a gloved hand being laid upon my arm, and a voice saying, with that tendency to run all the words into one which is a characteristic of a certain stage of intoxication, "H'llo ol'fler!"

I turned; there was a woman—a young woman and pretty one—so young and so pretty that her youth and prettiness seemed to lend to her condition an added horror. She was well but flashily dressed, and, already at that hour of the day, she was drunk.

When I turned and looked at her she regarded me with an imbecile smile.

"Don' you know me, ol' f'ler?" she said. I did not know her; I did not want to know her. So little did I want to know her that, with a view of avoiding an altercation with an intoxicated woman in Piccadilly, I stepped off the pavement with intent to cross the road. To my disgust, she followed, calling after me:

"Ol' f'ler!"

I turned to her.

"If you address me again I will call a policeman."

Whether she understood me or not, I cannot say. I doubt if she understood me clearly. The confusion and noise of the traffic, the condition she was in, these things were against her. I turned again to continue my passage across the street, and I imagine that she endeavoured to follow me. I say that I imagine, because I am not certain of what it was that exactly happened. All that I know is, that a moment afterwards there was a hubbub of voices, and a woman's shriek rang out, high over the din of the traffic.

"He's run over her!" some one shouted—shouted it, as it seemed, right into my ear.

When I looked to see what it was had happened, I saw that a rapidly increasing crowd was gathering in the centre of the street, and that it was blocking the traffic. All eyes were endeavouring to look at something which lay upon the wooden pavement.

It was that unfortunate woman. An omnibus driver, all his faculties bent upon a frantic endeavour to "cut out" a rival, had knocked her down, and the two wheels on one side of his heavily-laden vehicle had run right over her.

Poor creature! Though Heaven knows that I had not been in any way to blame, I almost felt—it was all so sudden and so awful that I almost felt as if I had had a hand in her destruction. I gave a constable my card, and requested him to inform the authorities of the hospital to which they were taking her—"all that was left of her!"—that I would call to learn how she progressed.

One may easily imagine that that little incident did not tend to remove the depression for which Ryan's loquacity had been primarily responsible. So it is that one may leave one's house in the brightest possible frame of mind, and yet, owing to circumstances over which one has absolutely no control, be in a condition of profound dejection within a distance of less than half-a-mile.

This reflection is not made under the delusion that it is in any way original, but it is so.

Hardly had I returned to my chambers in the afternoon

than I was informed that some one wished to see me. The some one proved to be an attendant at the hospital to which the unfortunate woman had been carried in the morning. He brought a very pressing, and what I thought a very singular message, to the effect that she wished to see me, adding, on his own account, that if I wished to see her alive I should have to go to her at once.

Although the woman was a perfect stranger to me, and, after all, had brought her fate on herself by her own misconduct, I could not but feel moved when I was told that to so young a creature, and to one to whom the future might have meant so much, life was to come to so sudden and to so terrible a close.

"Is it so bad with her as that?" I said.

"Well, sir, her nurse told me that it was even chances that she would be dead before I got back."

The man spoke respectfully, but with as much appearance of concern as if he were speaking of a pig.

I told myself that, if it were so, it would be useless for me, at considerable inconvenience to myself, to wait upon her message, since, before I could get to her, she would be dead. And, in any case, what could there be, of the slightest possible moment, which she could have to say to me?

I tried to learn from the messenger. "You understand that this person is, so far as I am concerned, a perfect stranger. You have no idea what it is she wishes to say to me?"

"I know nothing about that, sir. I only know what the message was I was to give you: that if you didn't see her before she died you would be sorry as long as you lived. The nurse said I was to tell you that those were the exact words she used."

I hesitated. Who was this woman that, for her sake, I should unnecessarily dye my thoughts a darker hue? Ralph was to call for me very shortly. In a pleasant frame of mind

for festivity I should be if I came fresh from a death-bed—
and such a death-bed—to the feast. If every drunken female
who chose to get herself run over were to claim the right to
summon me to witness her final moments, a fresh charm
would be added to the already numerous charms which enhanced the pleasures of existence.

The man perceived my hesitation.

"I must be going, sir. Is there any message I can take?"

The fellow seemed to take it for granted that I would
not go. I do not know if he detected on my physiognomy all
the inevitable characteristics of a brute. I groaned.

"You are sure that she is dying?"

He actually grinned.

"I don't think that there's much doubt of that, sir."

I don't know if he thought that I feared that there might
be doubts—he gave me that impression.

"Well, I'll come with you," I said. "I am pressed for
time, and I have an important engagement very shortly. But
I should not like any poor creature to go out of this world
thinking hard thoughts of me."

I summoned a hansom, and we went in it together.

I found that man a most interesting companion. During
the short ride from my chambers to the hospital he told me
more pleasant anecdotes about awful accidents than I had
ever heard in all my life before. He dwelt upon the details,
making vivid references to "pools of blood" and shattered
limbs. So that when the vehicle drew up before the doors of
the hospital, I felt as if I were about to cross the portals of
a building which had about it something of the nature of a
shambles or a slaughter-house.

I had no notion that I was about to assist at one of the
most eventful interviews of a long and not uneventful life—
so wholly devoid of anything in the shape of prophetic in-
sight are my poor eyes.

CHAPTER XV

"IN ARTICULO MORTIS"

"Not dead," they told us, when we reached the ward in which the woman lay.

A little further on the information was amplified.

"Not dead," said the nurse whose duty it was to attend on that particular patient, "but dying fast. You're only just in time."

"Is she conscious?" I asked.

"Quite conscious. In cases like this they often are. She'll probably be conscious to the very end." Then she added, as if in answer to an unspoken inquiry which she saw written on my face: "Nothing that you can say or do will make any difference to her now—except, perhaps, that it may ease her mind. It's internal hemorrhage—she can scarcely last half-an-hour at the most."

When I stood beside the bed on which the woman lay, I could see that what the nurse said was true, that nothing could make any difference to her now. Even to my unpractised eyes, upon her countenance the near approach of death was written large.

None of her injuries were visible. Whatever they might be, they had left her face untouched. It struck me, when I first had seen her, how pretty she was. Lying there, with her hat off, and her face just visible above the bedclothes, she looked prettier even than she had looked in the street. She never had been beautiful; there was not intellect enough in her face for that. But she was conspicuous, in an unusual degree, for that dainty, sensuous, animal prettiness, which experience has taught me that the majority of men find more attractive in a woman even than actual beauty.

One thing I was glad to notice, that there was about her no atmosphere of drink. All that had gone. The great thing that was coming had driven it away. So far as I could judge, she was as sober as ever a woman was. She was not to realise that drunkard's ideal: she was not to die drunk. I could see at a glance that she was as much herself as I was, if she was not more herself than I was.

We remained looking at each other for a moment in silence; I wondering what there was of such pre-eminent importance, as the message which had been brought to me suggested, which she could possibly have to say to me, a perfect stranger; she regarding me with her big, wide open, beautiful blue eyes, as if she were endeavouring to read on my countenance something which she fancied might be there.

As she showed no sign of any intention to speak to me, I spoke to her.

"I hope," I said, "that you are not in pain?"

The tone in which she replied was not loud; she was evidently very weak, and her voice was failing her as swiftly as her life, but it was clear, and cool, and self-possessed. She gave me the impression that she was saying what she meant.

"No; I am not in pain; I am dying." Then, after a pause: "I don't mind."

"I hope," I continued, "that, in what has happened, you do not think that I have been in any way to blame?"

"No. Besides, it doesn't matter."

The careless, and even cynical indifference of her words and manner, in circumstances such as hers, and in one so young, jarred upon one's nerves. I was at a loss what to say to her. Evidently this was a case in which none of the ordinary truisms would be of the least avail.

While I hesitated she went on of her own accord.

"I knew you this morning, though I was so drunk."

"You knew me?" I regarded her more attentively. I had not recognised her in the street; I did not recognise her then. "I do not remember ever seeing you before."

"No, perhaps not; but I've seen you before, and I know all about you, too. When they told me that you had left your card, and that I was booked, I thought I'd send for you, just to ease my mind."

As she uttered the last few words, the shadow of a smile wrinkled the corners of her lips, and gleamed out of the depths of her big blue eyes. It did not strike me as being a pleasant smile by any means.

"In what can I be of use to you?"

Candidly, I did not believe her when she said that she knew me. I was beginning to suspect that she might be a worse woman even than I had originally imagined. Her next words, therefore, took me aback.

"Did you know Mr. Philip Bennion?"

"Know him! He was my most intimate friend."

"I knew him too. And he knew me. And he didn't like what he knew of me either."

What could the woman mean? What could such as she have known of Philip Bennion?

"I fancy that you cannot be referring to the Philip Bennion with whom I was acquainted."

"Oh, yes, I am—don't you make any error! He used to live in the same place you do. He was a card! And he thought that I was another card."

I, also, was beginning to think that she was what she termed "a card," and a very queer card too, to be talking in such a strain when death was already touching her with outstretched finger.

"Who are you?" I asked. "What is your name?"

"You wait half-a-second. I'll tell you. I've got time. I know I shan't go off until I've told you. It was so that I might tell you that I asked them to fetch you here, just to ease your mind and mine."

Again a shadow of a smile flitted across her features. It was my imagination, perhaps, but it seemed to me that that smile made her look as cruel as the grave—that grave to which she so swiftly, and with such astonishing disregard of what there might be after, was hastening. I was at a loss what to say to her. I wished that I had disobeyed the summons, and that I had not come. Young and pretty as she was, there was something about her looks and about her manner which began to fill me with a sense of absolutely painful repulsion. Suddenly she asked a question: "Do you know Ralph Hardwicke?"

"Ralph Hardwicke?" I stared at her still more. Why did she want to drag in his name as well as Philip Bennion's? I fancy my manner was sufficiently frigid. "I know Mr. Hardwicke very well."

"I'm his wife."

Although I heard her words, I did not catch her meaning. It surely was not strange. I think that, for a moment, my senses were numbed. I looked at her askance. "You're his—what—?"

"I'm his wife—I'm Mrs. Hardwicke. I'm Ralph Hardwicke's wife."

To call the expression which momentarily transformed her countenance a smile would be absurd. It was a malignant grin. I gazed at her with horror. I had not the slightest doubt that she was telling an astounding lie. And that

a woman in her position could be capable of such an uncalled-for, such an atrocious, and, as it seemed to me, such
a senseless lie, was to me most horrible.

"You're Ralph Hardwicke's wife! Woman, with death
actually holding you by the hand, how can you tell me such
a falsehood?"

The only excuse that I could make for her was that she
might be delirious, but there was no symptom of anything
of the sort in her demeanour. She seemed quite calm—
calmer by far than I was.

"It's no falsehood; it's gospel truth—truer than any gospel I ever heard of. I'm Ralph Hardwicke's wife as safe as
houses."

If she was not raving mad, then she was the wickedest
woman I had heard or read of, and all that I could do would
be to hope that that mercy would be shown to her which
she would not show herself.

"Heaven help you, woman!"

I spoke out of the fulness of my heart. She answered
with that dreadful shadow of a smile.

"Put your hand beneath my pillow. You will find a purse.
Take it and open it. You will find in it my marriage lines. It's
better to have these sort of things in black and white, you
know; it's more convincing."

Mechanically, in obedience to her request, I inserted
my hand beneath her pillow. She herself was powerless to
move. The only things about her which were still alive were
her faint, clear voice, and her monstrous wickedness. I almost expected, so little faith did I place on any word she
said, to find nothing there. However, my fingers closed on
something. I drew it out. It was a purse; one of those gorgeous affairs which women, so it appears to me, for purposes of ostentation, love to carry in their hands. I know

not what other reason they can have for such curious behaviour.

"Shall I open it?"

"Don't I tell you to? Right at the back, by itself, you'll find my certificate of marriage. It's a copy, but you can always get a sight of the original if you would like to."

I did as she bade me. I opened the purse. In the compartment at the back, by itself, as she said, there was a paper. I took it out. I unfolded it. I looked at it. And, as I did so, the words upon the paper, and the paper itself, and the place, and everything, swam before my eyes. I never came nearer to fainting than I did just then.

The paper was a certificate of marriage.

It was, or it purported to be, the certificate of a marriage which had taken place some three years back at a registrar's office in the north of London, between Ralph Hardwicke, bachelor, and Louisa Pratt, spinster.

"This," I gasped, when I recovered breath enough to speak, "is either a forgery, or it relates to some other Ralph Hardwicke than the one I know."

"That's where you're wrong. You ask the Ralph Hardwicke whom you know. If he denies it—I don't think he will, but he might, if he knew that I was dead—you go up to that registrar's office, and they'll tell you all about it."

"But," I cried, "my Ralph Hardwicke's going to be married in the morning!"

The woman laughed. Already as good as dead, already face to face with the Great Unknown, she laughed. Such a laugh! The nurse, who was hovering about the bed, when she heard that dreadful sound, turned towards her with a startled air.

"My dear!" she cried.

But the woman paid no heed to the nurse.

"So's my Ralph Hardwicke going to be married in the morning. Shall I tell you who he is going to marry? He's going to marry Miss Macrae—pretty Nina! Do you think that I don't know? Why, I've known all about it from the first."

"But, if you are indeed Ralph Hardwicke's wife—and Heaven forgive him, and help him, if you are!—what devil's impulse has led you to cause him to think that you are dead?"

"To think that I am dead? Go along! He knows that I'm not dead. He knows that I'm as much alive as you are. It was only yesterday that he came to see me."

"Only yesterday that he came to see you!"

Was this some hideous dream? Would these things pass away? If but they would!

The woman continued speaking. She seemed to have acquired fresh strength for the sole purpose of adding to my torture. She spoke with more animation than she had yet displayed.

"It's like this. I'd done something of which he knew, and for which, if he liked, he could have put me away—quodded me, you know. And if I made myself disagreeable he'd have done it, too, as soon as look at me—I know Ralph."

She laughed again. Good heavens, what a laugh it was! Sometimes, to this hour, I still seem to hear it ringing in my ears.

"So, as he'd made it all right in the money way, I didn't care who else he married. He might have married half-a-dozen more wives for all I cared. I should rather have liked him to, because then I should have a chance to get my knife in him."

Could these things be? Could Ralph Hardwicke, that paragon of all the virtues, my ideal strong man, have all the time been the thing this woman pictured him? Clean-souled, clean-thinking, clean-living Ralph? Could he have been an infinitely baser thing even than a Raymond Clinton?

My brain reeled at the mere contemplation of such a possibility; of all that it entailed. I was stunned, dazed. My heart seemed broken. I never realised, till then, that Ralph Hardwicke had been every whit as much my boy as Philip Bennion's.

"Tell me," I said at last, for the woman continued watching me with her big blue eyes; "if all that you say is true, how came you first to know him?"

"I'm 'the Pet of the Peris,'" she said.

I stared at her with bewildered eyes. Her words were as double Dutch to me.

"You're the what?"

"You don't know much. When I first knew Ralph Hardwicke my name was on every wall in town, in letters as long as your arm, 'The Pet of the Peris!' At this very moment there isn't a music-hall in London where they wouldn't give me twenty pound a week for a two-song turn, and glad to get me at the price! And here am I, just dying. I'd have gone back long ago if it hadn't been for Ralph. He said I wasn't to, and though I'd have given a finger off my hand to go, I didn't dare. It sounds funny, but it's true."

"You mean that you were a music-hall singer?"

"I mean that I am 'the Pet of the Peris.'" She repeated the words with an obvious pride in them which was as curious as, under the circumstances, it was ghastly.

"And—and did Mr. Hardwicke see you in the exercise of your profession?"

"He came to the hall where I was singing—he was always coming there—and, one night, some one brought him round and introduced him to me just as I had done my turn.

That was on Tuesday, and on the Thursday we were married."

I failed, for a moment, to quite grasp the meaning of her words.

"On the Thursday you were married? Do you mean that you were married after only four-and-twenty hours' acquaintance?"

"That's about the size of it. I knew all about him before I knew him. I thought it was good enough, so I broke off my contracts—weren't there ructions! Ralph had to pay up all round—and we were married."

She paused. Then, as I sat too bewildered and horrified to speak, she went on again. But I noticed, even amidst the agony and confusion of my mind, how faint her voice was growing, and how her life was ebbing fast.

"If you don't think that was like him, you don't know Ralph Hardwicke. If he sets his mind upon a thing he'll have it, though all the devils in hell should try to stop him."

She gave a little cough—a little choking cough. The nurse came swiftly to her. She put her hand beneath the patient's head and raised it from the pillow. She carefully wiped away a crimson stain which, all at once, had dyed the woman's lips.

The woman spoke again:

"I'm Ralph Hardwicke's wife."

And she was dead.

CHAPTER XVI

NOT ASHAMED

How I reached home I am unable clearly to state. I have a dim recollection of stumbling down the hospital steps. I think I called a cab, but, at the same time, I am not sure that the hansom was not waiting for me in which I had arrived. I know I did drive home, and I know that, as I drove, I kept pressing my hand against a paper which was in the breast-pocket of my coat. That paper purported to be a certificate of a marriage which had taken place between Ralph Hardwicke and Louisa Pratt.

Dewsnap, my servant, received me when I returned. He told me that I was late, and that my dress-clothes had long since been waiting for me to get into them. I said that I should not require them that night, because I did not intend to alter my attire. He looked at me askance, asked if I was not feeling well, and reminded me that Mr. Hardwicke was about to call to take me out to dinner.

"Leave me alone," I said, I am afraid querulously. "I am quite aware that Mr. Hardwicke is going to call."

Dewsnap left me alone, though I have no doubt whatever that he perceived that something out of the way had happened. They have the eyes of hawks, those servants!

I sat in a sort of stupor. I realised something of what the feelings of a man must be who is waiting for execution. It is possible, if he feels as I felt, that he may become impatient for the hour to arrive. It had to be. Why did not Ralph hasten, so that we might have it over?

I dared not think of Nina. My pretty Nina!

At last he came. I heard his vigorous step without; I

heard his hand upon the handle. I knew that he had opened the door, and that he was looking into the room. But, on a sudden, I fell into such a fit of trembling, that, at the first moment, I could not turn and face him.

His strong yet musical voice rang out across the room—

"Hallo, Otway, aren't you ready?"

Still I could not look upon his face.

I suppose that my behaviour struck him as strange. It was unlike me, when I received a guest, to sit crouching in a corner, with my back turned towards the door. He advanced further into the room.

"I say, do you know what time it is? Are you asleep, young man?"

Then I turned. As I raised myself from my chair, I felt that my knees were trembling beneath me.

When I looked at him I was struck more than ever by the strength and the beauty of his face; the intellect that was written large; the unmistakable signs of exceptional mental force and power. I felt as if he had been the accuser and I the accused. Far rather would I have had it so.

"Ralph," my voice still faltered, "I have seen your wife!"

There was silence—that awful silence which most of us have known at some time or other in our lives—that silence which is so infinitely more eloquent than speech.

As I raised my eyes to again look up at him, I saw that, during that interval of silence, his face had become transfigured. The change which had taken place in it would be difficult to describe in words—changes which take place in the expression of a person's countenance not seldom are. It betrayed no emotion, no surprise, no dismay, no sort of passion, but in an indefinable manner, it had become hard, and cold, and set, as if carved in stone; the face of a man all intellect, keen, razor-edged, as unyielding and insensible to outward influence as finely-tempered steel.

"So!"

That was all he said, and he moved to the fireplace.

"Ralph," I almost screamed, his passionless calm seeming to throw oil upon the flames which burned within me, "don't stand like that. Have you nothing to say? Don't you hear me tell you that I have seen your wife?"

"I hear you. Is she outside?"

"Outside?" I echoed.

"If she is outside, pray ask her to come in."

"She is not outside."

"Not outside?"

He stood looking at me with an insolent coolness which affected me more than any other behaviour on his part could possibly have done. What stupefied me with horror, he seemed to regard, if one might judge from his outward demeanour, with almost complete indifference. I found myself wondering, for the first time during all those years, what manner of man he really was.

"Well," he added, "have you anything else you wish to say?"

"Is it possible, sir, that there is nothing which you wish to say?"

"Oh, yes, there are one or two things. By the way, aren't you coming to dinner?" He looked at his watch. "It is on the table."

"Is that the only observation you have to make—that dinner is on the table?"

"You are really too severe, and, after all, one must dine."

"As you say, one must dine."

He stood regarding me in silence for a moment or two. Then he asked a question:

"Do you intend to forbid the banns?"

"Forbid the banns?"

"I mean, do you mean to place any active obstacles in the way of my marriage with Nina in the morning?"

"You—you ineffable villain!"

"Don't call me names! I mightn't like it."

"Not call you names! Is it conceivable that you think that, knowing what I know, I will allow you to go to the altar with Miss Macrae, and allow you to pledge yourself to be her husband in the sight of God and man?"

"Then you mean to tell Nina—that I have a wife?"

"I mean not only to tell Nina, but I mean to publish it to all the world. It is not expedient that men like you should be married and folks not know it. It should be published from the housetops, so that he who runs may read."

"Don't be melodramatic. What's the use? Be easy!" He looked at me with the most indescribably insolent air of amusement. "I fancy that you mean to be worse than the other."

"Than what other?"

"Than old Ben!"

I gasped.

"Do you mean that Philip Bennion knew that you were married?"

"Certainly. I told him all about it. It was the queerest marriage of which you ever heard." I quite believed him. "I didn't go much to music-halls, even in those days. They always struck me as stupid. They bored me! But one night I dropped into the Aristophanes, and I heard 'the Pet of the Peris'—has the little darling told you that she was known to the world as 'the Pet of the Peris'?"

"She has."

"She always tells every one five minutes after she begins to speak to them. Well, I heard 'the Pet of the Peris.' Such a voice! And such songs! You never heard such—harmony! But, on the other hand, you never saw such limbs—and, you know, she showed them. There lay, from an artistic point of view, her chiefest virtue. When she came upon the stage to sing—forgive the word!—her second song, I made up my mind that I would have her. The more I saw of her, you know, the more I wanted. So I went the next night, and the next, and the next—all to see 'the Pet of the Peris'!—and I think it was the night after that that I was introduced to her. I took her out to supper, and I offered her marriage. I had heard what sort of woman she was, and I saw for myself— for, even in those days, I had discerning eyes—that nothing else would serve. So I offered her all I had to give for all that she had to give. She accepted the offer, being quite well aware that she would have the best of the bargain, and the day but one after we were married. Well, in about a week I was sorry, painfully sorry. And as, in my excessive verdancy, I couldn't see my way at all, I came and made a clean breast of the whole affair to dear old Ben."

"And what did Philip Bennion say when you told him such a tale as that?"

"He did not make the exhibition of himself which you are making, and which you bid fair to make hereafter. But then he was a cleverer man all round."

This young man's insolence was really most amazing! To listen to him, and to look at him, one would have thought that he had been discovered in as common-place, every-day a little adventure as ever man yet had. A mere nothing at all!

But as he continued, something began to come into his

voice which suggested that there was in him, somewhere deep down, a white-hot heat of passion which burned and seared every fibre of his being.

"Old Ben's advice was, to have no scandal, to make the best of 'the Pet of the Peris,' to keep her, as much as possible, out of sight, and to go on as if she wasn't there. This was all very well in theory, but in practice it wouldn't work. For the mischief was that I had loved Nina ever since I was a boy."

"You say that you loved Nina ever since you were a boy, and yet you did this thing!"

"Precisely. There's the puzzle. What they call the psychology of life's a riddle. You, with your limited powers of comprehension, will not understand me when I tell you that it was because I loved Nina, that I did this thing. It was because I loved Nina, that I married 'the Pet of the Peris.' But what I had not realised was, that I should love Nina all the more because I had married 'the Pet of the Peris.' But that was what actually happened. And that was where the mischief all came in."

He was silent for a moment. When he spoke again, although he did not raise his voice above his ordinary tones, his words seemed to scorch me as they issued from his lips.

"You may thank your stars, Otway, that you are a man of little passions. If you have no raptures of enjoyment, you have no agonies of baffled yearning. If you desire a thing you do not long for it with ever-increasing longing, until you realise that between you and madness there is but a slender veil, which may be severed at a touch. I do. When I desire a thing, my desire grows and grows, until I must have what I desire—or go mad. When I was still a child I realised that with me this was so. So I learned to put a continual restraint upon myself, until I had at least acquired the art of concealing the strength of my desire. Nature, and the social conditions under which we live, compelled me to become a thing for which, I assure you, I have no more taste than you—a hypocrite.

"You will perceive that I have an acute perception of the character, and situation, of Joseph Surface.

"Directly I had married that husk of a woman, that drinking, swinish, mindless animal, Nina's figure rose up in front of me in contrast to the figure of the creature I had made my wife. I had always loved her. My love for her became a sort of madness. I saw what I had lost, what I had done. I verily believe—I am aware that similar language has issued from hundreds of thousands of meaningless mouths before, but I use it with full appreciation of its meaning, I think you will grant it when I go on—I verily believe that no man ever loved a woman as I loved Nina—loved her! As, my God! I love her now! There was nothing I would not have done to win her. I would have run the gauntlet through all the devils in hell."

Ralph Hardwicke was unconsciously quoting the awful words which had been almost the last to issue from his dead wife's lips.

"A shrewder man than Philip Bennion was, perhaps never lived. I was amused when, that day, you asked me if I thought that he was mad. His chief fault, in my eyes, was that he was too sane for me. He soon had a good idea of the sort of thing that was going on inside of me. You see, he was a student of character, and he understood me, not only better than any one else, but almost as well as I understood myself, and he loved me although he knew me for what I was. There was only one thing he would not have sacrificed for me. That one thing was Nina. He had agreed to keep my marriage secret, but he had not bargained for my making love to Nina. So he sent me right away, and told Nina that I was not for her, and that she was not for me."

When he said that I started, and he perceived I started.

"Yes, I see what you are thinking of. You are right. Nina told the truth when she said that old Ben had warned her off me. It was I who lied. My dear fellow, it is not the only lie which I have told you—it is only one out of perhaps more than a thousand. It is one of the misfortunes attendant on the exigencies of such a situation as mine, that I am constantly constrained to lie."

He spoke of the absence in himself of any moral sense as calmly as if he were expounding the intricacies of an abstruse problem in mathematics.

"When old Ben interposed it already was too late— with all his acumen he had not plumbed all the depths that were within me. My desire for Nina had become the master passion of my being. It was my one idea. I had already told myself that I would have her, let the price which I should have to pay for her be what it might. So soon as old Ben dispatched me on my travels I set to thinking by what means I could attain the object of my desire."

Ralph Hardwicke paused. He drew a long breath. He seemed to hesitate. But perhaps that was only supposition on my part, because, directly afterwards, he went on with a cool, calculated precision of utterance which held me spellbound.

"I realised one thing—that I should never have Nina while old Ben could keep her from me. That Philip Bennion blocked the way. But, with crass stupidity, there was another thing I did not realise, and, what is even stranger, it is only quite recently that I have begun to realise it. It is incredible, but it is true. I did not realise that the shortest way to obtain possession of Nina was to kill my wife."

He said this as quietly as if he had been requesting a light for his cigar; but he said it in a manner which caused every drop of blood in my body to suddenly congeal. "Ralph!" I cried.

And something made me shrink from him as if he were some awful thing.

He regarded me with a smile of indescribable amusement, evidently wholly unmoved by the state of agitation I was in.

"The idea, my good fellow, would have been obvious even to you—I see it, as they have it, in your eye. To have killed my wife would have been to resolve, at the smallest possible cost—practically, as you yourself perceive, at no cost at all—the situation to a T. It would, henceforth, have been all plain sailing. Old Ben would have been satisfied. As I told you, and as, for once in a way, I told you truly, the dream of his existence was that Nina and I should be man and wife. If I had only been able to furnish him with proof that 'the Pet of the Peris' was no more, he would have bidden me God-speed, and given me his blessing there and then. Nothing could have been more satisfactory—nothing simpler. But—Otway, I hope you won't be shocked, you really are so funny. In matters such as these you should eschew sentiment. Look facts in the face with the indifference with which you perceive the elementary fact that two and two make four. But—and now my blindness seems to have been almost miraculous, for I can assure you that no one could have gone about the business more coolly and logically than I did—but, the one idea, the only idea which occurred to me, was to kill old Ben. I thought that if he was out of the way——Now, Otway, what is the matter?"

The matter was, not that I had fainted, or lost my senses, but that my legs had given way beneath me, and that I had fallen helpless to the floor. He advanced as if to proffer me assistance.

"Keep away! Keep away!" I screamed, in a sort of strangled whisper. "Don't touch me!"

He seemed surprised that I should shrink from his touch as from the touch of some evil thing.

"My dear fellow, don't be absurd. I have no wish to touch you against your will—why should I have? Only you don't look very comfortable, huddled up in a heap upon the floor. And an old man like you! If you decline my assistance, don't you think that you had better make some attempt upon your own account to assume a position more becoming to your age and character?"

"You devil!" was all I said.

He laughed.

"Be it devil, if you will have it devil—why not? The word conveys but a vague and fanciful meaning to my mind. Perhaps it conveys a clearer meaning to yours—I am content. If my conversation annoys you—far be it from me to knowingly bore any one, and least of all, my dear old fellow, would I bore you—I will cease. Only I imagined, as I might be able to throw some light upon a subject in which, I believe, you have shown interest, that you would wish to hear me to the end."

I heard him to the end, not because I wished to, but because I could not help it. Because he held me spellbound. Because, as he unfolded, as it were, inch by inch, his monstrous wickedness, wickedness of which I had thought—and I had seen something of the wickedness of men, and women too—no human being could have been capable, I hung upon his words, so that they held me with the fascination with which the mesmerist holds his subject.

As he stood looking down at me, handsome as Lucifer,

as Milton's Satan, and, surely, scarcely less wicked, I staggered to my feet and tottered into a chair, and he went on, speaking for all the world as if he were narrating some admirable little story, which it was really worth my while to make a note of.

CHAPTER XVII

AN ARTIST IN MURDER

"IF the mere idea of killing dear old Ben pains you, how much more, at its first inception, must it have pained me! As I told you—once more, truly—I loved old Ben, with the one exception of Nina, better than anything in the world. And, though you may be incredulous, I have a capacity for love which very few men possess."

To hear this fellow speak of love. Was there ever such prostitution of good words!

"When I first realised, or, rather, in my blind stupidity, thought I realised that the only path to Nina lay over Philip Bennion's grave, I almost resolved to give her up. I did so resolve, for a time. But I found that to keep my resolution was beyond my strength. To some men, to the majority of men, the thing would have been easy. I am differently constituted to the ordinary run of men—it was impossible to me. I could not live and give up Nina. So I determined, as the lesser of two evils, dearly though I loved him, to sacrifice old Ben.

"Having arrived at that determination, I considered how best to carry out the task which was before me.

"You told me, as I dare say you have not forgotten, of a conversation which you had with Philip Bennion on the night before he—died. You told me that the subject of the conversation was 'Murder, Considered as One of the Fine Arts.' I don't know if you are aware of it, but that was a favourite subject of his. He often spoke of it, and, unconsciously to himself, inspired me with the ideas which were ultimately to lead to his own destruction.

"He had always believed, as he himself told you on that last night, in what he called the Artist in Murder. He had maintained over and over again to me, that it was quite possible for a cool and clever man to commit murder, without leaving behind him any traces of a crime. You remember when you spoke of that conversation to me, I told you that Philip Bennion's ideas upon the subject were all very well in theory, but were impossible in practice—medical science was too advanced. I told you so, as you will yourself perceive, for obvious reasons. In reality, I not only thought that they were practicable, I had proved they were. I had perceived their practicability when Philip Bennion first broached the subject. But I never thought, at that time, that I should ever put the matter to the test of actual experiment."

He paused again, and while he paused, to use that old hack phrase, I seemed to hear my own heart beating. He stood looking in front of him, with an expression on his face as if he were endeavouring to recall to his mind the proper sequence of events. There was nothing in his looks, or about his bearing, which would have led any one for one moment to suppose that this man was confessing a murder of which he never once had been suspected—as black and foul a murder as ever yet was done.

He went on speaking as quietly and indifferently as if he were referring to some trivial matter with which he himself was not in any way connected—while I, as I listened, scarcely dared to draw my breath.

"I studied the literature of homicide, in a general sense, as far as I was able. I saw at once that the chief point to be considered was to kill, and yet to leave no trace of a crime. That was the crux. If you did that, you did all. And I soon perceived that, if books were to be trusted, in Italy, during the sixteenth century, and thereabouts, the main object of the aspiring homicide was continually attained. The means used, in such cases, was invariably poison. In literature, at any rate, the Italian poisoners were proverbial.

"It was not to be overlooked that, since those days, science had advanced. Detection of crime by scientific methods had become the standard topic, for instance, of the newspaper leader writer, and of the sensational novelist. The Italian poisoners, one might say, were not detected because, in their days, science was in its infancy. In these days of exact, unerring, scientific analysis, their deeds would have been made as plain as the sun at noon.

"Was this so?

"I turned my attention to toxicology. I read the works of the latest authorities on poisons, among others the works of Mr. Lewis Cowan."

As he mentioned Mr. Cowan's name, Ralph Hardwicke smiled.

"The result was, that I came to the conclusion that science, in its impartial onward march, had helped the criminal quite as much as it had helped the detective, and that it was just as possible to poison a man, without fear of detection, as it had ever been.

"The Italians were remarkable, not only for the poisons which they used, but also for the manner in which they conveyed their poisons to their victims. The modern, vulgar poisoner invariably poisons the victim's food, or medicine, or drink, or, at any rate, something which he puts into his stomach.

"In a case of illness the first question always asked is, what has the patient ate or drunk? Post-mortem examination reveals it. And so, in nine cases out of ten, you have only to look at the recorded cases. The poisoner simply gives himself away.

"The greatest Italian artists never poisoned either food or drink. They never allowed their poisons to go into the stomach. They injected them either into the finger by means of a ring, into the arm by means of a bracelet, or into the neck by means of a necklace. They resorted to more ingenious and delicate methods even than those.

"I had gone to study the Italian poisoners upon their native heath, and it chanced one day that I was passing through the Fiezza Palace with a Roman Cardinal, when, in one of the private apartments, he pulled up short, and called my attention to a cabinet. That is the identical cabinet standing in the corner there."

Ralph Hardwicke pointed to what Mr. Vose had called the Medici cabinet.

"He told me, that Roman Cardinal, that few people ever came into that apartment, and that that cabinet was never shown to visitors. He lied. Whether consciously or unconsciously I cannot say—but he lied. And it is chiefly because he lied that I am now, my dear Otway, treating you as my father confessor. I will not say that your discovery of a previous Mrs. Hardwicke has had nothing to do with the matter, I will not go as far as that; but certainly I should never have told you what I am telling you now if that Roman Cardinal had not lied in saying that that cabinet was never shown to visitors.

"Nina had been in Rome the year before, and some fool or other had taken it into his head—I only learnt this too late, that fatal too late, my dear fellow, which we are all of us destined, some time or other, to hear—I say that some fool or other had taken it into his head to show her over the Fiezza Palace. This fool was a friend of old Ben's, was himself a bric-à-brac hunter, a man well known in Rome, and he introduced Nina to the Fiezza Palace for the sole purpose of showing her this cabinet. He not only told her in what its peculiarity lay, and so on, but he lectured on it, so far as I can understand, for about two hours in the middle of a broiling summer's afternoon. Not only so, but he actually gave her a photograph of the cabinet. I have seen it, she has it still. And what with the photograph, and that old fool's prosing, and the legends which he told her of the dreadful deeds which that key had done, she has never forgotten that cabinet from that day to this. What that has to do with the sequel you will see.

"Directly I saw the cabinet and heard about the key, I said to myself that this was the very thing that I was looking for. If I could only plant that cabinet upon old Ben, he would soon cease to be a factor requiring consideration.

"But it was not such an easy thing to do, to plant that cabinet upon old Ben. First of all, I had to get it out of the Fiezza Palace, and that did not look easy; and then I had to insinuate it into old Ben's possession without allowing him, or any one else, to suspect that it ever, in any sense, had been in mine.

"I managed to do the first thing—I managed to get it out of the Fiezza Palace. I have found that in Rome you can do a good many things with money, and it cost me a surprising sum of money to get that cabinet out of Pontifical keeping. The next thing I had to do was to entrust it to a dealer for sale, with instructions that he was only to sell it to a particular person, and then for a song. The key he never had. It was never in his possession. He never saw it. He was as innocently unconscious of there being anything peculiar about the cabinet as a babe unborn. I instructed him to tell the purchaser that the key required cleaning and that it would be forwarded after the cabinet had been sent home. I imagine that that dealer thought that I was making a present with that display of eccentricity which is peculiar to Englishmen—and I let that dealer think. As a matter of fact, he was right. I was making a present—after a fashion of my own.

"That accommodating dealer took a little shop in the Brompton Road, his stock-in-trade consisting principally of that cabinet. So soon as he had settled down a little, I mentioned, casually and privately, to old Ben that I had noticed in that part of the town what seemed to me a new dealer in curiosities. Exactly what I expected would happen did happen. A new curiosity shop was to old Ben what the smell of a fox is to a hound—he followed the scent as soon as he struck it. The next day he visited that dealer's shop, and the day after that the cabinet came home.

"Old Ben was *in excelsis*. So was I.

"Before that cabinet made its appearance in England I had visited the East, and had there made some very peculiar and some very striking experiments with certain poisons which—I happened to hear of. One in particular had appealed to my imagination as being, like the cabinet, just the thing I wanted. I arranged with its discoverer—I believe the gentleman I refer to can really claim to be its discoverer—whose residence at that time was at Cairo, to forward me, at a moment's notice, to an address in London, a certain quantity of this—article, which was to be freshly distilled, and which was to be contained in an air-tight cover.

"Before the cabinet came home I wired to Cairo, and my wire was attended to with a really surprising celerity and punctuality. I charged the key, and I sent it, of course as coming from the dealer, to old Ben.

"As, I believe, my dear old fellow, Mr. Cowan has informed you, and you are therefore, without my telling you, aware, it was a peculiarity of that particular poison that it lost its potency by being kept. When fresh from the still, less than a drop injected beneath the skin of a man, no matter where, would kill him as if by a flash of lightning. It's a fact. If you doubt it, try it—in the interests of the spreading abroad of the truth, and the advancement of science. But this virtue—for such, in my eyes, I need not observe it was—became diminished when the stuff grew stale. It required more and more of it, and it took longer and longer to kill as the days, and even the hours, went by. Until, finally, it wouldn't kill at all, not if you injected a whole hogshead.

"It had left the still quite long enough by the time that it reached me. I had calculated—since I had been careful to arrange that the cabinet should come to old Ben locked—that, directly he got the key into his hands, like a child with a new toy, he would not rest until he had unlocked it. I took it for granted, in other words, that, certainly within half-an-hour of the receipt of the key, he would be dead.

"I knew by what post the key would reach him. I took care to appear on the premises within half-an-hour of the post's arrival—half-an-hour, that is, after it was in. I expected to find old Ben departed, and my idea was to slip the key out of the lock, and to put in its place a harmless *facsimile*. Before I had gone to bed that night that peculiar key would have been improved out of existence. It was the most beautifully planned thing of which you ever heard.

"Unfortunately, as the poet too truly remarks, 'the best laid plans of mice and men aft gang agley.' My 'best laid plan' went all 'agley.'

"When I arrived, instead of finding old Ben a corpse, I found that he'd gone out to dinner. Some ass had come, just as the post was in, and insisted upon hauling dear old Ben off with him, then and there. I couldn't ask about the key—how was I to know anything about it?

"You can take my word for it—on this occasion you really can—that I did not spend a pleasant night. The next morning, as soon as decency permitted, I trotted round once more. This time I found old Ben roaring and raging, and calling down all the curses of all the gods upon Ryan's head, and upon that dealer's head, and upon the man who had hauled him out to dinner's head, and upon everybody else's head. Old Ben had lost the key! My beautiful key! My best planned key! The key over which I had spent days, and weeks, and months, and which had cost me—my dear fellow, what that key had cost me, from first to last, I shouldn't dare to tell you. He had put it—somewhere, and old Nick alone knew where.

"We hunted for the key, dear old Ben, and Ryan, and I. I assure you that I was as keen in the chase as any one. But we never found it. You may fancy my sensations. I trotted round here every day, sometimes half-a-dozen times a day. I took it for granted that old Ben would find it, perhaps in his waistcoat pocket or some equally impossible hiding-place, and that he would there and then proceed to slaughter himself at some wholly unexpected and most inconvenient moment. It would just have been like old Ben."

This man, Ralph Hardwicke, told all this with smiles, as if he had been recounting the finest joke in the world. But, all at once, he ceased to smile, and there came again instead that curious intensity of passion, which was all the more noticeable because it was suggested rather than expressed.

"And that key never was found, until you found it, although Nina thinks it was. Ah, Otway, there's the mischief! If it were not for what Nina thinks, ten thousand Philip Bennions might rot before you would wring a confession out of me, and before you would be able to place your finger on a clue which would lead you to the solution of my crime.

"Mind, I have exchanged no plain words with her, but I know what is passing, and what has been passing in my darling's mind. I know that she recognised that cabinet when first she saw it, and that she would, there and then, have betrayed her recognition to Philip Bennion if it had not been that he had told her that it was I who had called his attention to the shop in which it had been purchased.

"Otway, it is not the least curious part of this my really curious story that I verily believe that, from the first, Philip Bennion knew me for what I am. I have no positive proof that this was so; but he was, as I have said, the shrewdest man I ever knew, and the more I look back at the things which have gone, the stronger my conviction grows that he knew from the first that I was a man who would stick at nothing to gain a desired end.

"More; although I know that he never told her I was married, when he saw how I longed for her, I do believe that he dropped her a hint that under no circumstances could I make her my wife, and that he dropped her a still further hint that I was the sort of man to leave no stone unturned, either in heaven or in hell—in spite of circumstances—to make her mine. Again I have no positive proof that this was so; but I believe that that is what he did.

"When Nina saw that cabinet, and recognised it for what it was—with Philip Bennion's hints still rambling in her breast—when he told her that it was I who first had set him on its track, I believe that her tongue was paralysed and that her blood ran cold.

"Otway, I find it hard to believe, and unfortunately still harder not to believe, that the woman for whose sake I was willing, nay, eager, to steep myself to the lips in sin, suspected me all along to be the base thing which indeed I am.

"I say that I find that reflection hard. One likes a woman whom one loves as I love Nina, to think that one is at least—a man. I know, although in so many words she has not told me so, that Nina believes that I placed that cabinet in Philip Bennion's way, for the purpose for which, in fact, I did. That she believes that, after all, he found the key, that it slew him, and that I am his murderer. I imagine that that belief has only come to her, as the proverbialist has it, 'line upon line, here a little, and there a little'; but I know that she believes it wholly now. And it is chiefly because of her belief—because she has lost her belief in me—rather than owing to the little discovery which you have made, that I am throwing up the game on which I had staked my all, which I had almost won, and which I, after all, have lost.

"Kismet. It was written in the skies."

He paused; then he said as coolly and unconcernedly as he had spoken yet:

"Otway, I did kill Philip Bennion."

That finished it, when he made, with cynical calmness, his hideous confession.

I had hoped, when he had spoken of the loss of the key, that, through no merit of his own, but through the mercy of his Maker, his hands were free from the actual stain of innocent blood. That, as by a miracle, he had been saved from guilt worse than the guilt of Cain. That for him, even yet, all was not lost. That there was hope for him, even upon earth, through the cleansing fires of repentance.

But when he said so quietly, and so indifferently, that he indeed had killed the man who had held him dearer than a son—and for nothing, just no cause whatever—I would rather I had died, for I, too, loved him as a son.

For my heart went out to him even as he stood there. I loved him even in that dreadful hour. What is it in some men which makes us love them, even though we know them to be villains as black as ever were spawned from the mouth of hell?

"Some men, when the seed which they had so hopefully planted, and so carefully tended, had come so utterly to grief, would have resolved to plant no more, to turn their attention to some other branch of agriculture; in fact, to take a beating. Owing to a constitutional defect of my nature, I am not—to my misfortune—a man like that. I am, I assure you, hard to beat.

"When I perceived that there was no likelihood of that key being found, and knew that if it were found it would—from my point of view—be of little good, I tried again. I turned my attention to another poison, also a product of the East. They are quite amateurs in the compounding of poisons—*dilettanti,* even in the present year of grace—in the districts which I vaguely call the East. And at least some of them are poisons which, as I happen to know, are not included in the British medical pharmacopœia.

"This poison had one characteristic which the other had—it killed at sight. So to speak, at less than sight. In other respects it differed. Its destructive qualities were not evanescent, it would kill at a hundred years of age just as well as in its early youth, and it left behind it absolutely no traces of the work which it had done. The other poison did leave traces. That is to say, when you had conducted a post-mortem on the body of one man whom it had killed, you might, possibly, perceive its presence in another, as, probably, Mr. Lewis Cowan told you. With this it was impossible. You might examine the bodies of a hundred of its victims, and wholly fail to perceive any generic suspicious peculiarity which was common to them. It simply produced valvular disease of the heart, and that, I believe, is pretty generally recognised to be a 'natural' cause of death. You see, therefore, that the doctors were right on at least one point at the inquest—Philip Bennion did die of valvular disease of the heart."

Again he paused. And again, when he went on, his tone became more earnest.

"Had I known—clearly understand me—had I known what I know now, Philip Bennion might have lived, so far as I was concerned, until he had attained the age of a Methuselah, had I had the faintest notion that Nina suspected that I meditated murder with the aid, and by means of, that dainty cabinet of yours."

"I knew it from the first!"

A voice interrupted him. A voice which so filled me with amazement that I was roused, on a sudden, out of the state of prostration, mental and physical, into which I had fallen.

It was Nina's voice. Nina Macrae, unnoticed both by Hardwicke and by me, had come into the room.

CHAPTER XVIII

HOW PHILIP BENNION DIED

SHE was standing just inside the door. Her eyes were fixed upon Ralph Hardwicke with a look in them which, if he felt towards her one-half of what he said he did, must have scorched him to the soul.

"I knew it from the first," she said.

He shrank away from her as if she had struck him an unexpected and a stunning blow.

"Nina," he cried.

She turned to me. She asked a question.

"Do you believe in visions?"

"My dear!" was all that I could stammer.

"Because, as I was sitting just now in my own room, I heard Ralph"—with what a bitter emphasis she pronounced the word, and how she shivered as she uttered his name!—"talking to you here. I could not hear what was the subject of his conversation. But something told me that he was speaking of Philip Bennion's death. And something made me put on my things and steal out of the house as if I were a thief, and come to claim, as my right, on this the eve of my wedding day, a share of my betrothed husband's confidence. And, I perceive, it is well I should have come."

She turned upon him with an intensity of scorn of which I had not thought that she was capable, and which penetrated even Ralph Hardwicke's hide-bound front. He lost something of his air of cool assurance and ready presence of mind; he became sullen and dogged; looking like a man who, brought unexpectedly to book, anticipates a whipping, and resents it.

"Go on," cried Nina. "Do not let me interrupt you. Pray continue as if I were not here. You were saying that the weapon with which you killed Philip Bennion was the poisoned key of that wicked cabinet. Well, I tell you that I knew that from the first. What next?"

"You imagined that you knew; you allowed your imagination to run away with you. I did not kill him with the key."

"At a moment such as this, at a moment of such perfect frankness, is it still necessary that you should lie to me?"

"It is no lie. I did not kill him with the key. I killed him with something else."

"With something else? You hear this man?" She pointed to Ralph Hardwicke with a gesture which made him go white to the lips. "This is the man I—love!"

There was a break in her voice as she uttered that last word, which seemed to strike a chord of uncontrollable desire in Mr. Hardwicke's bosom. Visibly trembling, he advanced to her, his hands stretched out to her as if to take her in his arms.

"Nina!"

Shrinking back, she waved him away from her with a movement of self-abasement, of profound repulsion, which seemed to overwhelm him with amazement.

"Do not touch me! Do not pollute me further! Already you have smirched me with stains which never shall be cleansed. Tell me," she added, after she had paused a moment, as if to regain some fragments of self-control, "what was this insurmountable obstacle which guardian told me kept you from me, and which, in your judgment, necessitated Philip Bennion's removal from your path."

The scorn with which her voice was filled; the bitterness which made each word stick like a barbed arrow in Ralph Hardwicke's quivering flesh!

He replied to her with an air of savage sullenness.

"The obstacle to which you allude was a trivial one. It was a wife."

"A wife? Whose wife? I do not understand you."

"No? And yet it is sufficiently plain. I happened to be married already."

"You happened to be married—already?"

"Exactly. I happened to be married already. And Philip Bennion happened to be aware of it; and I happened to want to make you my wife in spite of the existence of a previous Mrs. Hardwicke. There you have the situation in a nutshell."

"You were married! And you asked me to be your wife!"

As the full meaning of Mr. Hardwicke's words became clear to her comprehension, she seemed to be turning into a statue of stone.

With some feeble idea of relieving somewhat the tension which racked my brain, half-mechanically, and certainly with no clear consciousness of what it was that I was doing, turning, I took up a pipe which lay among several others on my mantelshelf. I was, just in the same semi-automatic fashion, about to fill it with tobacco from my tobacco-jar, when Mr. Hardwicke noticed my action. Moving quickly forward, before I had any idea of his intention, he took the pipe which I designed to smoke clean out of my hand.

The manner in which the thing was done, even more than the thing itself, took me by surprise. A moment before he had seemed to be shrivelling up before the lightning blast of Nina's righteous scorn; all at once he was alert and full of life again.

"Permit me," he said.

He asked for my permission, but he did not pay me the

compliment of waiting to receive it. He snatched the pipe from my hand without giving me the chance of answering either yes or no.

When he got it he stood turning it over and over, and regarding it with a very curious smile upon his face.

"Wasn't this old Ben's pipe?"

I started. It was! Oddly enough, in my bewilderment of mind, I had chanced to take up from my mantelshelf the very pipe which had been lying by Philip Bennion's side that morning on which Ryan and I had found him—dead. Taking it up from where it lay on the floor, I had borne it away with me there and then. I had not expected, then, ever to obtain a memorial of my friend from Raymond Clinton. I had resolved, therefore, upon the spur of the moment, to obtain one on my own account.

I carried it with me, intending to regard it as a relic of our lifelong friendship. A relic found under memorable circumstances. The last pipe which he had ever smoked.

Coming straight from the dead man's presence, with his pipe in my hand, I had placed it on my mantelshelf among the other pipes which were there, intending later to give it a place of honour. It had continued on my mantelshelf, untouched, until, as if by chance, my hand had strayed its way.

It was a fine pipe, meerschaum, finely coloured, curiously carved; just such an one as Philip Bennion would have valued. Ralph Hardwicke continued turning it over and over, almost, as it seemed, with an air of pleased recognition.

"May I ask where you got this from?"

"I found that pipe lying by the dead body of the man you murdered. It is the last pipe which Philip Bennion ever smoked."

He actually glanced up at me and smiled.

"Ah! So—so it happened, after all? At times I almost wondered—principally because I could find no traces of the pipe. I thought, at first, that thief Ryan must have stolen it. But then it did not seem to be quite likely, since he went on living. And all the time it has been lying on your man-telshelf. How blind are the children of men! Do you know, my dear Otway, that on one occasion your drunken friend, Mr. Raymond Clinton, caught me, in the small hours of the morning, looking for this identical pipe? I could not make out where it had gone. But he was so very drunk that I think he mistook me for a ghost."

I remembered Mr. Clinton's confused and incredible story of his having seen Philip Bennion's "ghost" bending over the open drawer in the writing-table. I remembered, too, how I had found the drawer still open and its contents disarranged when I had gone to look at it. Could he have been so far gone in intoxication as to have mistaken Ralph Hardwicke living for Philip Bennion dead? If so, then great indeed must be the power of alcohol!

While he had been speaking, Mr. Hardwicke had filled the bowl of the pipe from the contents of my tobacco-jar. He pressed the tobacco into its place with the nice care of the man who appreciates an easy-drawing pipe.

"I gave this pipe to dear old Ben; hence, my dear Otway, my immediate recognition of its familiar form. It was a mark of my affection and esteem. Not a bad pipe, is it?"

He held it up so that we might see it to complete advantage.

"It is better even than it seems. I doubt if there is such another pipe in all this curious world. I did certain things to this pipe in accordance with a prescription which I received—for a price—from a certain 'dealer in magic and

ₔ a pipe bewitched; I cast on it a spell. l gave to it a
ₔssession—the possession of the key which unlocks
ₔₜₑ of—is it life or death? The psychologists still argue.
Otway, I spoke to you of the second poison which I lighted
on when the poisoned key had failed. Nina, you have been
under the impression that the key of that charming cabinet
was the weapon with which I worked my wicked will. You
have been wrong. This is the plaything with which I killed
old Ben."

Holding up the pipe in his left hand, he pointed at it
with his right. I shrank still farther from him. Nina covered
her face with her hand. She cowered. Her tall form bent.
She seemed to crouch on the ground.

Our demeanour appeared to afford Ralph Hardwicke
nothing but amusement. He went on, in a light, bantering
tone:

"Only a pipe—only this and nothing more—and yet so
great a thing. My dear Otway, I have reason to believe that
two questions have much exercised your mind of late. The
one: Who killed old Ben? The other: How he died? I will
resolve for you both problems. It was I who killed him. And
this is how Philip Bennion died."

There was the sound of a slight scratching. I looked up.
He had struck a match. He was advancing the stem of the
pipe to his lips. I rushed forward. I sprang at him.

"Ralph!" I screamed.

With a quick movement he evaded me. I grasped nothing but the air.

"My dear old fellow, what would you do? One would
think that you don't wish to know how Philip Bennion died.
But I know you do. See—like this."

The horror of that moment! I live in it again even as I
write.

I stood, rooted to the ground, as if my limbs were paralysed. I was conscious that Nina had removed her hands from before her face, and, with a new sense of fear, was looking towards the man who had professed to love her. Ralph Hardwicke stood in front of her, in all his youth, his beauty, and his strength. A smile parted his lips. A light, which I believe from my soul to have been the light of madness, was in his eyes. He thrust the pipe into his mouth. He raised the flaming match. He applied it to the bowl. A faint transparency of smoke issued from his lips. And he fell dead.

A single whiff of tobacco—innocent tobacco—taken from my own jar—scarcely one whiff!—drawn through that devil's pipe had knocked the life right out of him, had slain him as if by a bolt from heaven.

He had shown us—while Nina and I looked on—in his own person, how, taken unawares, in a second of time, just as he had been commencing to enjoy what had been to him one of the chiefest pleasures of existence—a pipe of tobacco—Philip Bennion had died.

CHAPTER XIX

THE END

It is not so very long ago, if one counts by the mere flight of time, since first Philip Bennion and then Ralph Hardwicke died. And yet it seems as if it had been a century ago—as if, indeed, there had always been that black cloud behind. And yet, in another sense, it seems as if it were but yesterday since I stood there with Nina, and, in the full flush of his young manhood's strength, saw Ralph Hardwicke die. I fear that in that sense it will always seem as if it were but yesterday.

We hushed it up, the whole dread story. In that we were able to do so much as that, we need give thanks. Save Nina and I, no one knows just how Ralph Hardwicke died. Certainly none has the least suspicion of that strange history of wickedness which one would scarcely dare to say was human, which he had to tell, and to which, whether I would or I would not, I had to listen. That same night, in my own fire, I burned that hideous pipe. I stood by and watched it till it was utterly consumed. Only Nina and I are aware that there was ever such an instrument of murder, and of sudden death. It is a secret which we shall carry with us to our graves. The Medici cabinet now stands again in Rome. But it is now fitted with another key, which more closely resembles the keys of every day. The former key, that "ingenious contrivance," has vanished with the pipe.

Raymond Clinton is still in full chase of those fabulous animals, yclept the dogs. I fancy he will overtake them before he's done. Ryan has found another place, with me. I think he is a better servant to me than he ever was to Philip Bennion.

I no longer live in Piccadilly Mansions. I occupy a house of my own. With me resides Nina Macrae. She says that she will never marry. Possibly she never will. She declares that I am the only husband she will ever have—I,—a broken-down old man! And, sometimes, when she sits at my feet, and pillows her head upon my knee, and a great silence seems to wall us round, I know that she is thinking of what I am thinking, and of what, strive against it how I may, it seems that I am forced to think—of how her other guardian, the friend of my boyhood, died.

Lightning Source UK Ltd.
Milton Keynes UK
UKOW051136260413

209821UK00006B/266/A